The apartment

Mack Bolan slipped inside, the Beretta tracking the dark interior. His combat senses flared suddenly, and the soldier ducked.

An assailant jumped him, and the Executioner cursed. In his hesitation, he'd silhouetted himself against the light in the hallway.

Bolan dropped flat and swept his opponent's legs with a circular kick. A body hit the floor hard, and the soldier slapped the wall several times before finding a light switch.

When the lights came on, the Executioner stood pointing his pistol at the head of a woman on the floor. She stared back at him over the barrel of her own gun.

"Put it down," Bolan growled.

"No way," the woman retorted. "I guess we have what you Americans call a standoff."

MACK BOLAN ®
The Executioner

DON PENDLETON'S
THE EXECUTIONER®
WAR BIRD

A GOLD EAGLE BOOK FROM
WORLDWIDE®

TORONTO • NEW YORK • LONDON
AMSTERDAM • PARIS • SYDNEY • HAMBURG
STOCKHOLM • ATHENS • TOKYO • MILAN
MADRID • WARSAW • BUDAPEST • AUCKLAND

To all the members of the German *Polizei*—
for bravery and unswerving dedication
even in the face of mortal danger

First edition February 2000
ISBN 0-373-64255-5

Special thanks and acknowledgment to
Jon Guenther for his contribution to this work.

WAR BIRD

Copyright © 2000 by Worldwide Library.

Printed in U.S.A.

Imagine that leader of all the enemy, in that great plain of Babylon, sitting on a sort of throne of smoking flame, a horrible and terrifying sight. Watch him calling together countless devils, to despatch them into different cities till the whole world is covered, forgetting no province or locality, no class or single individual.

—Saint Ignatius of Loyola

I refuse to stand by and watch the enemy dispatch terrorism, striking at the innocent. When that happens, I will dispatch a justice of my own kind, and repay evil with fiery retribution.

—Mack Bolan

THE
MACK BOLAN®
LEGEND

Nothing less than a war could have fashioned the destiny of the man called Mack Bolan. Bolan earned the Executioner title in the jungle hell of Vietnam.

But this soldier also wore another name—Sergeant Mercy. He was so tagged because of the compassion he showed to wounded comrades-in-arms and Vietnamese civilians.

Mack Bolan's second tour of duty ended prematurely when he was given emergency leave to return home and bury his family, victims of the Mob. Then he declared a one-man war against the Mafia.

He confronted the Families head-on from coast to coast, and soon a hope of victory began to appear. But Bolan had broken society's every rule. That same society started gunning for this elusive warrior—to no avail.

So Bolan was offered amnesty to work within the system against terrorism. This time, as an employee of Uncle Sam, Bolan became Colonel John Phoenix. With a command center at Stony Man Farm in Virginia, he and his new allies—Able Team and Phoenix Force—waged relentless war on a new adversary: the KGB.

But when his one true love, April Rose, died at the hands of the Soviet terror machine, Bolan severed all ties with Establishment authority.

Now, after a lengthy lone-wolf struggle and much soul-searching, the Executioner has agreed to enter an "arm's-length" alliance with his government once more, reserving the right to pursue personal missions in his Everlasting War.

PROLOGUE

The telephone on his desk buzzed for attention. It was his private line, and few people had the number. Even fewer would know to call him there at that hour. It had to be the call he'd been waiting for. He stepped away from the picture window of his penthouse office and walked quickly to his desk.

He picked up the extension and dropped into his chair. "Yes?"

"It's me."

"You are late," the man said, leaning back in the chair and propping his feet on the desk. "Where have you been?"

"Making the final preparations. It looks as if the project will be completed on schedule."

"And the Americans?"

"They bought it," came the reply. "They believed every word. We've been tracking their agent's movements. I imagine he will have quite a surprise awaiting him here in Frankfurt."

"I imagine so," he said.

The thought of *that* news eased his discomfort. He considered asking if they knew the identity of the CIA agent who would attempt to rescue Dr. Vasec Krizova, but then it didn't really matter. Krizova would cooperate in working toward completion of the project. He was certain their reluctant benefactor wouldn't cause any trouble. He had no qualms about carrying out the threat he'd dangled over Krizova's head.

Although not before their objectives were completed.

Everything was moving on schedule and according to plan. In fact, he couldn't have asked for anything better. Success was a part of his life. Everything he possessed was the result of his own hard work—his spacious penthouse office; the expensive furniture; the fine clothes he wore. His suits cost more than some fine furniture, and he was chauffeured in cars that were rotated out twice a year. All of his material possessions were the realization of a long-held dream.

His office looked upon most of the city of Frankfurt. Ah, yes…Frankfurt, an icon of cultural history. To him, the city made the ultimate statement about the German people. It was a population that had experienced misery in its most abject forms, yet the German people always managed to survive, returning to the well of prosperity a little bit stronger each time.

The ideals his grandfather had instilled in those great German terrorists of the seventies were the same principles and foundations of his own organization. However, there was also nothing wrong with having a lot of money. Money and power went hand in hand, and he was rapidly gaining both. His company was now one of the largest and wealthiest operating within the European Union. The business practices of the cold war era were obsolete in his Germany of tomorrow.

One day, the boot-lickers of his government would hang from the heights of Frankfurt, and their American allies would swing beside them. He fully intended to destroy the Western swine on their own turf—kill them in their own beds while they slept. Men. Women. Children. Americans were all the same to him—fresh meat, lambs to the slaughter. His family had inherited the legacy of the wolf, and he would carry it out until his death.

"You have done well, my friend. I am very pleased."

"I live only to serve you, great stone god!"

He smiled at the reverent title. Yes, he truly was a god, and nobody would dare oppose him. He would lead his followers to victory. He would see to the completion of the project, and then he would exact his revenge.

Nevertheless, for now, the plan called for the completion of the project. He would demonstrate his true might and authority. He would pass on the legacy, and pay the Americans back in blood for all they had done to his country. German power would rise again. It wouldn't be the Fourth Reich.

Simply a call-to-arms for those who deserved the inheritance.

1

Frankfurt, Germany

Mack Bolan saw the gunmen in time to avoid the hail of bullets.

He executed a shoulder roll and came up in a crouch, his Beretta 93-R out and ready for action. He thumbed the selector switch to fire 3-shot bursts and squeezed the trigger. Two rounds took the first gunman high in the chest, while the third slug tore away his throat. The impact spun the gunner, his Uzi machine pistol flying from numb fingers. He fell onto the hood of a nearby car and slid to the concrete.

The sound of gunfire was thunderous inside the underground parking garage of the Frankfurt airport. Bolan scarcely had time to draw his weapon from the trunk of his car, left there by arrangement with Stony Man Farm's contacts in Frankfurt. There hadn't been time to grab spare clips, and the appearance of two more enemy on his left flank made him consider the ammunition situation.

It wasn't good.

Bolan moved the selector switch to single shot as he sought cover behind a nearby minivan. He fired again, and the 9 mm Parabellum round punched through the second gunman's gut. The man was lifted off his feet, then he hit the concrete with a dull thud.

As the Executioner turned his attention toward the remaining pair, a black Mercedes squealed around a far corner of the garage, carrying five more men. The odds were hardly even, but the Executioner wasn't concerned. The odds had been stacked against him before, and as long as there were rounds in his weapon, he was ready for them. Flame spit from the Beretta's muzzle as the next slug hit the jaw of Bolan's closer opponent, and a well-placed shot to the chest dropped the gunman's partner.

Bolan sprinted back to his own vehicle, yanking a small bag full of additional clips from the trunk before getting behind the wheel. He turned the key in the ignition, and the little Citroën's engine roared to life. Bolan stomped on the accelerator and backed out of the space, tires smoking and screeching. The Mercedes ground to a halt, and men bailed out of the sedan as the soldier put his car in Drive. One of the gunmen raised his machine pistol before realizing he was too late. The bumper struck the gunner at midthigh, shattering his upper leg and throwing him into his partner.

The front-seat passenger ordered his men back into the Mercedes.

Bolan's eyes flicked to the rearview mirror as he headed for the exit. He accelerated smoothly on the straightaways, rapidly descending through the garage. He knew they would pursue him—whoever the hell *they* were.

When Bolan hit street level, he used his limited German to find the signs that would lead him to the autobahn. This was unfamiliar territory, with the enemy in close pursuit. He needed to put distance between himself and his pursuers—make it look as if he were trying to escape. He couldn't run forever, but the soldier needed some room at that moment. When the time was right, and there were no innocents to get in the way, Bolan would show his hand.

The chase continued onto the autobahn, and the Mercedes slowly closed the gap. Bolan knew the Citroën would never outrun the luxury sedan, but he kept the pedal to the floorboards. He watched the enemy draw closer in the rearview mirror, formulating his plan. He needed to find a deserted road, and the answer appeared up ahead in the form of a secluded exit. Bolan jerked the wheel at the last moment, churning dust and gravel in his wake. The Mercedes driver powered his vehicle into the turn smoothly, continuing the relentless pursuit. The driver was a professional, which meant the well-armed passengers were probably pros, as well.

Bolan made a hard right and proceeded another half mile before jamming on the brakes and cranking the wheel. The Citroën shuddered to a halt in the center of the road, and now faced the approaching Mercedes. Bolan popped the trunk and went EVA. He grabbed a combat harness from the trunk, slinging it over his shoulder, then retrieved a silenced Heckler & Koch HK53.

The soldier left the roadway and entered dense foliage on his right. Most of the sun had disappeared behind the horizon, and the woods were dark. He kept low, avoiding overhead branches as he moved deeper into the forest. After he'd covered twenty-five yards, he crouched and slipped into the load-bearing harness. Multiple weapons of war hung from the harness, including several fragmentation grenades, two incendiary grenades and spare ammunition for the Beretta. The .44 Magnum Desert Eagle hung in military webbing on Bolan's side. He chambered a round in the HK53 and waited quietly.

Now it was time to even the odds.

The Executioner could barely make out the shadowy figures in the twilight of the roadway. He could hear them more than see them, and the leader was definitely shouting in German. Bolan couldn't understand what the man was saying, but he was aware of the brief silence that followed. Professionals or not, the men were apparently reluctant to put themselves at unnecessary risk. This was the Executioner's element. If the enemy was going to play his game, it would have to play by his rules.

Bolan concentrated on listening and breathing. The men were stomping around, grumbling and cursing as branches whipped their faces, and twigs cracked under their weight. There would be a total of four, including the leader. His pursuers now had the advantage of darkness, as well, provided they knew how to use it.

Bolan still had surprise.

He stayed motionless as his first target passed within a couple of yards. The soldier was a ghostly wraith as he rose to his full height and triggered the HK53. The extractor ratcheted in the darkness as Bolan pumped five rounds into his opponent. The 5.56 mm slugs tore through the gunner's body at a velocity of over 300 meters per second. Bolan immediately ducked and crawled forward as bursts of autofire from the others drilled into the gunman. The bullet-riddled corpse dropped to the forest floor.

Bolan could hear excited cries as the gunners rushed to where their comrade had fallen. He considered lobbing a grenade, but it was risky given the darkness and his proximity to them. It would be better to take them one at a time. There was a brief conversation between the pair before the third man appeared nearby and whispered a curt order. They ceased talking immediately and fanned out. Their leader was obviously no amateur.

One man faltered off to the left, while his partner proceeded directly toward Bolan's position. The soldier reached up to his webbing and drew a Ka-bar fighting knife, waiting as the enemy drew closer. As soon as the gunman had passed, Bolan rose and grabbed the man by the throat with one viselike hand, the other driving the knife blade up through the base of the skull. He eased the body to the ground, wiping the blade clean on the dead man's shirt.

The Executioner sheathed the knife, and hefted his HK53 again. He stayed low, slowly turning to face the enemy. One of the men was approaching. Bolan remained in a crouch, waiting until the enemy was on top of him before he stroked the trigger. The rounds tore through the gunman's belly and chest, tossing him against a nearby tree. He crumpled to the ground in a lifeless heap.

Something brushed against the soldier's leg less than a second before a rigid forearm encircled his neck, yanking him backward and virtually hanging him in a sleeper hold. Bolan twisted his head and drove his arm upward, trying to insert a hand between his neck and the crook of his assailant's arm. Stars danced in front of Bolan's eyes as he began to lose consciousness. He abandoned his maneuver for another, gripping the stock of his HK53 and driving it backward into his adversary's shin. The hold slackened, and Bolan wasn't about to let the advantage slip away. He gained his feet, straightening the arm that had been choking him, and yanked downward as he rose. The elbow snapped. Bolan used the broken limb to whip the man around, slamming him onto his back. The soldier dropped his knee onto his attacker's solar plexus, then smashed the windpipe with a rigid knifehand strike.

The man's screams died in his throat.

Bolan got unsteadily to his feet, taking a moment to catch his breath before he searched the bodies for identification. When his task was complete, he quickly made his way back to the road.

The Mercedes was empty. Bolan found what looked like only registration papers inside the glove box, but he took them anyway. After quickly looking around, the soldier pulled an incendiary grenade from his harness, yanked the pin and tossed the bomb inside the Mercedes. The interior of the vehicle burst into flames as he got into his Citroën. He could hear approaching sirens in the distance and had no desire to deal with the police. He had reached the autobahn entrance before the Mercedes's gas tank ignited. The sedan exploded into flaming bits of twisted metal, and a cloud of thick black smoke rolled into the starless sky.

The Executioner had been in Frankfurt less than an hour, and somebody had already tried to kill him. He had some questions that needed some answers.

And Mack Bolan fully intended to get them.

SO FAR, BOLAN'S MISSION hadn't gone as planned.

Brognola had said that the President didn't want to draw attention to this mission. So much for that.

Dr. Vasec Krizova was one of the most respected and renowned scientists in the world of modern air warfare. The Czechs were proud of their brain child, and his reputation had never been made a secret. His design plans to a new kind of combat stealth fighter would put America at the top of the list for air superiority, and well ahead of the competition—not that they weren't close to that already.

According to Stony Man Farm intelligence, Krizova was selling to the highest bidder. Krizova's weak spot was apparently geared not to his own wealth and notoriety, but to the well-being of his daughter. He wanted her to attend the best schools, to have a slice of the good life. Anyone who could make that happen would be in the running to lay hands on the new jet design.

An unknown party had originally approached Krizova with a rather generous offer, but the scientist refused to sell for reasons that were equally unknown. The U.S. was the next to come forward, but its approach to the whole thing had been less conspicuous. The President's advisers had suggested that open bidding by the U.S. was asking for trouble. It would draw unwanted attention, as well as a slew of attempts by other factions to steal the information. The offer was made through a group of Japanese businessmen, who agreed to buy the information and secretively resell it to the U.S.

Something had gone wrong.

At the meeting in Prague, the CIA agent assigned to facilitate the meet and oversee the exchange, Carter Wiley, had disappeared, along with Krizova and his daughter. The Japanese businessmen had been found inside Krizova's home with their throats slit. Both the Czech Republic and the Japanese people were pointing fingers at every major world power. They were particularly upset with the United States, and the CIA headquarters in Frankfurt was screaming for help. Wiley had been one of their best agents.

According to Hal Brognola and Aaron Kurtzman, Stony Man's cybernetics wizard, a large part of the jet fighter's capabilities were still on "a need-to-know" basis, but the things whispered in certain political circles made even Bolan think twice. Supposedly, the fighter was faster and more powerful than anything on the drawing board, and bits of intelligence revealed it was years ahead of other designs the military was currently working with. In the wrong hands, it could be an extremely dangerous weapon. If a fanatical group laid hands on the design plans, or even compelled Krizova to help them build the aircraft, they would truly have the rest of the world at a disadvantage.

The Executioner was in Frankfurt for two reasons.

One, it was the logical place to start. Two, by the President's orders, he had the complete support of the CIA, who could explore avenues Bolan didn't have the time or resources to tackle alone. The original thought had been to start in Prague, but the soldier dismissed the idea. Something just didn't feel right. His instincts told him Frankfurt was where the answers would be found, and he had learned to follow those instincts.

As Bolan drove the Citroën into the heart of the downtown, he weighed his options. A check of his watch confirmed his meeting with the CIA contact was still a couple of hours away. He had enough time to check into the hotel, but he needed to get rid of the rental car. Descriptions of him and his vehicle would be reported to whoever had ordered the airport attack on Bolan. He was realistic enough to know he couldn't maintain a low profile. Eventually, the enemy would find him and try another hit. In the meantime, he would do what he could to keep them off balance.

Bolan had visited the city on other occasions, and he estimated he was about three miles from the hotel. He pulled over and parked his car on a dark side street. He packed his duffel with spare clips for the Beretta, then stowed the remainder of the gear in the empty tire well under the carpeted floor of the trunk. He locked the vehicle, quickly found a stairwell down the block and descended the stairs to an underground platform.

Germany had one of the most efficient public transportation systems in the world. The U-Bahn was an efficient network of trains that shuttled people from one district to another. It was the grandfather of subway systems around the world, the interconnecting miles of rail extending from central stations in Frankfurt and Berlin, then stretching out like crooked fingers to the most remote parts of the country. Arrival and departure times were accomplished with near perfect accuracy.

Bolan dropped some coins into a machine, which obediently spit out his ticket. The train arrived a few minutes later, and the ride to the district of Konstablewache—constable plaza—took just under ten minutes.

Bolan checked into his hotel under his Mike Belasko alias. Thanks to Aaron Kurtzman, his credentials were in perfect order. His cover documents stated he was a businessman for a major television company, and he was there to attend the conference being hosted at the hotel. Nobody appeared to give him a second glance.

The soldier quickly showered, then donned jeans and a worn flannel shirt. He slipped into his shoulder holster, checked that the Beretta was locked and loaded, then went to the window and looked out onto the city streets fifteen stories below. He decided a recon of the area where he was to meet his contact would be a good idea.

He took the elevator to the lobby, opting to take his room key with him. He didn't want the staff to be aware of his movements. Bolan walked the few blocks to where the meet was scheduled. He didn't have a name, just an address and a vague description of his contact.

The meeting area turned out to be a five-story apartment building on a quiet residential street crammed with vehicles parked on both sides. He studied the front of the building before using one of the keys left in the rental car to open the lobby door. The vestibule was dank and narrow. Bolan could barely make out the tired, checkered linoleum under his feet and the chipped paint on the walls as he quietly climbed the stairs. The apartment building was designed with the steps in the front half, and each landing had two doors facing it that led into the apartments.

Bolan reached the fourth floor and stopped.

The apartment on the right was where the meet was to take place, and its door was ajar. Bolan immediately whipped his Beretta into play, thumbing off the safety and catfooting to the door. He managed to open it wide enough to silently slip inside. The Beretta tracked the dark interior, and Bolan listened for a sound or evidence of movement. Nothing but dead silence greeted him. He could barely make out a room on his right in the dim street light coming through a far window.

His combat sense suddenly tingled, and Bolan ducked. An assailant was on him, and Bolan cursed. In his hesitation, he'd silhouetted himself against the light of the hallway. His attacker had obviously committed to the charge before the Executioner ducked, ramming a knee into his shoulder that had probably been intended for his groin. Bolan regained his balance, dropping to the floor and sweeping his opponent's legs with a circular kick. A body hit the ground hard, and Bolan slapped the wall several times before finding a light switch.

When the lights came on, the Executioner stood pointing his pistol at the head of a woman on the floor. She stared back at him over the barrel of her own pistol. She was young, with a sharp and sassy look. Her hair was the color of cocoa, and soft brown eyes glinted fiercely at him. She was sprawled on her back, but there was no mistaking the intent look.

"Put it down," Bolan growled.

"You first," she shot back.

"I never shoot a woman, unless she's trying to shoot me."

"Then I guess we have what you Americans call a standoff."

2

Commander Dortmund Linger was rather pleased with himself.

The project was on schedule, although Linger had learned long ago that trouble usually struck when things were proceeding as planned. He had learned many things as a former BND agent. The collapse of the Berlin Wall had ended all official tensions between the East and West, but there were remnant factions scattered throughout Europe that would have preferred to keep those hostilities alive.

Linger had no such agenda.

He was, first and foremost, a soldier to the cause. He was also a fugitive—there was no such thing as retirement for a cold war agent, other than the permanent kind. Men with his kind of skills were relics in the modern world of the so-called civilized politics and governmental negotiations. Linger had plied his trade elsewhere, with phenomenal success. He had been building his reputation for many years, first recruiting his group for work in South Africa, then extending into the larger market of mercenaries. The work had included everything from military coups to corporate espionage and sabotage. He had worked for Russians, Asians, Europeans and even guerrilla units in Central America.

Money was the center of his focus, and the principal factor in his successful creation of an army of elite mercenaries called the Iron Skull. Money motivated him, and it kept his men obedient. Linger had no use for the material gains of wealth, unless it somehow furthered the cause. It bought the best weapons, equipment and soldiers. It was also the common thread in his recent alliance with Edel Schleyer.

Linger's talents were invaluable to a man like Schleyer, but those talents came with a high price tag. Schleyer was respected in the international business world, with a nearly unlimited cash supply, but Linger questioned the man's sanity. Each one of Linger's men was loyal to their commander, and they understood Linger's vision. Not the "great inheritance"—that was Schleyer's vision. Linger envisioned killing as an art of survival, and his leadership skills were honing them into a crack paramilitary unit.

As long as Schleyer could pay, Linger and his men would provide a service. It was really that simple.

Keeping Krizova on schedule hadn't been a tremendous challenge anyway. There was no question of either Krizova's expertise or his genius. The Czech scientist had demonstrated his capabilities with admirable results, but he looked down on men like Linger. It was the age-old conflict of brawn versus brain that created unspoken hatred between Linger and Krizova. The mercenary considered himself intelligent, and Krizova was nothing more than a minor irritation to him.

Providing the resources necessary to complete the project had turned out to be another thing entirely. It was only Linger's connections with the underworld, and his previous business contacts, that had gotten the project this far. Those resources were quickly depleting, and Linger wasn't nearly as concerned with the project's timely completion as he was with the success of the undertaking.

Linger had also considered the personal risks. He wasn't worried about them, but he was quite aware of them. His

BND counterparts were close—he could practically smell them. Linger had been there for the meeting between Krizova and the Asians. It wouldn't be long before they found the body of the CIA agent. The mercenary had been careful not to leave evidence of his handiwork, but someone would soon figure out he was involved. He hadn't survived this long by underestimating the enemy, and it would be suicide to do so now.

An armored Hummer rolled to a halt, its black plating gleaming under the bright lights of the underground complex. The operations to clear enough rock and reinforce the complex with tempered steel beams and walls had taken nearly a year. The complex was buried beneath Frankfurt, and accessible by several of the abandoned tunnels originally designed to serve the U-Bahn system. The structure was nearly one hundred meters square, and there were anterooms beyond those measurements.

Linger stepped from the Hummer, walking to the rear and flipping back a canvas cover. He turned and motioned for a nearby group of guards armed with Uzi machine pistols to begin to unload aluminum cases of various sizes. The interiors of the cases were padded to protect the vital electronics contained within. He smiled as the men began off-loading the containers. Acquisition of these items signaled that the final phase of the project could begin.

Linger spun on his heel and marched his six-foot-six frame across the complex. He was lean and muscular, his broad shoulders tugging at the leather jacket he wore. Khaki fatigue pants were tucked into shiny combat boots. The mercenary stopped short to look up at the monstrous construction scaffolding.

There she sat, her wings stretched out like those of some great prehistoric bird. The sharp lines in her sleek black hull shone dimly in the bright lamps, witness to her untainted grandeur. Linger inhaled deeply, breathing in the essences of her spirit. She was a virgin weapon of war, a statue of destructive power, shadowing the men working around her like a great mother eagle protecting her young.

Linger lowered his blond head, his gaze coming to rest on the back of a short man dressed in a garish lab coat. The man was bent over a long table with a slanted surface, its top covered with schematics and sheets of paper marked with mind-boggling chemical and mathematical equations. Linger's eyes narrowed as he stemmed the sudden feeling of revulsion. He despised Krizova, and he fought the urge to pull the Mauser Model 80SAV pistol from under his right arm and shoot the man in the back.

Linger silently moved up behind the scientist.

Vasec Krizova turned with a start and found himself staring into Linger's chiseled features. The mercenary towered over him and smiled as Krizova fought to regain his composure. Genius or not, Krizova was a coward, and the mercenary had no respect for such men. Even at the time of his kidnapping, Krizova had cowered in the corner with his daughter as Linger's men murdered the Japanese and the CIA agent.

"Good evening, Doctor."

"Dammit!" Krizova spit, pushing up his bifocals. "Why must you always sneak up behind me? You are an uncivilized cur!"

A knife blade rasped from its sheath on Linger's belt.

"Watch your tongue," he warned softly, holding the knife centimeters from Krizova's lips. "You are not so valuable that I won't cut it from your mouth."

Krizova was intimidated at first, but he quickly regained some composure. "I'm not sure Herr Schleyer would appreciate that."

"Perhaps," Linger replied after quick consideration, "perhaps not. In either case, do not challenge me." Linger

returned the knife to his sheath as quickly as he had drawn
it.

"Have you brought the equipment I requested?" Krizova
asked.

"It is being unloaded as we speak," Linger said, snapping his head in that direction. "As soon as this is accomplished, I must contact Schleyer with an update. What is
the status?"

Krizova turned his back on Linger and studied the plans
in front of him with resolute skepticism. "It would be going
much faster if I had the proper personnel. Most of your
men are incompetent, and quite inept with their hands."

"My men are soldiers, not common laborers," Linger
said, sneering. "You would do well to remember that."

"And you would do well to remember if I have to resort
to building the entire cockpit section myself, it could have
quite an effect on your timetable."

"That is not my problem."

Krizova turned to face him again, smiling from ear to
ear. "I think your employer would feel differently."

"Do not take it in mind to complain to Schleyer," Linger
whispered. He leaned in close, the lights in his gunmetal
blue eyes boring into Krizova. The threat in his voice was
implicit as he added, "There is always your lovely daughter
to think of."

Krizova's complexion paled. Linger had struck a nerve.
Mila Krizova was being held at Schleyer's secluded fortress, and she was their one true bargaining chip. Only the
threat of harming her gave them the upper hand. Linger
knew he had to use that fact sparingly. If Krizova ever gave
up hope for her safety, things would come to a grinding
halt. Abuse of their hostage would only strengthen her father's resolve.

Linger whirled and walked away. He could feel Krizova
staring at his retreating form.

He was headed back toward the Hummer when a soldier rushed up to him. The man tossed Linger a smart salute, and Linger returned it.

"What is it, trooper?"

"Sir, we have just received a report. Lieutenant Volk's unit…" The soldier's voice faltered.

"What about Lieutenant Volk? Speak up!"

"S-sir, Lieutenant Volk's unit was defeated," the soldier stammered.

Linger fought back a wave of shock, and a burning sensation hit the pit of his stomach like a white-hot coal. Volk's unit had been sent to take out the American agent coming to investigate Krizova's disappearance. Volk had been one of Linger's oldest and most trusted unit leaders, and a damned good soldier.

"What the hell do you mean by this?" Linger demanded. "Are you trying to say an entire unit of armed men was no match for *one* CIA agent?"

"Sir, one of the men survived," the soldier replied, trembling slightly. "Grubel, sir. He said the American tried to run him over, and this agent fought more like a soldier than an intelligence operative."

"A soldier?" Linger echoed.

"That is what Grubel reported, sir. He's in the infirmary now, if you wish to speak with him."

Grubel would receive a medal and a financial bonus. Linger always rewarded bravery in combat. It kept his men loyal to the greater cause. This American agent, however, was another matter. Linger didn't need to hear any more details. He knew his units were comprised of capable, professional soldiers. He had handpicked every one of them. No ordinary CIA agent would have been able to defeat such men so readily. There was something definitely amiss in their original intelligence, and Linger fully intended to find out what that something was.

"Captain Hess!" Linger roared.

A tall, lean man wearing a side arm and the group's khaki fatigue uniform left his supervision of the equipment unloading, and rushed over to where they were standing. Niktor Hess had served under Linger for many years, first in the BND as a liaison, then with the mercenary group in South Africa. He was a crack leader, and Linger's second-in-command.

"Yes, Commander!" Hess barked.

"Gather six of your best men with full gear and return here in five minutes. We have a mission, and I am personally going to lead it."

"Yes, sir!" Hess departed to carry out his orders.

After Linger had dismissed the other soldier, he continued across the complex and headed toward the armory. He would have preferred to take a full complement of ten men, but he couldn't spare them. More than half of his private army had been retained to guard Schleyer's fortress, which also had a large area inside the land perimeter the group used for training. The remainder was needed here to keep the project on schedule.

It didn't matter. Under his observation, and Hess's able command, they would find the CIA agent. Linger would make his personal business to teach the American swine there were consequences to interfering with the Iron Skull.

It was a lesson he was looking forward to teaching.

EDEL SCHLEYER STOOD in the watchtower of his castle and stared into the vast sky filled with stars. His breath crystallized in the brisk night air. October was a beautiful and festive time of year in Germany. Autumn brought parties, celebrations and grand dinner balls, such as the one hosted by Schleyer earlier in the evening at his city home. After the guests had gone, Schleyer was driven to his fortress, about an hour's journey south of Frankfurt by car.

He now stood on the highest point of the fortress, taking in his breathtaking surroundings. He was truly the master of all he surveyed. The castle had been constructed in the 1600s by Duke Leopold von Heusen. Schleyer's grandfather had purchased the castle in 1900 to celebrate the arrival of the twentieth century and the wealth he had attained during his early years in business. The elder Schleyer had managed the large land deal at the peak of his career, and now Edel Schleyer owned both the castle and surrounding land.

Still, he felt empty.

His country was in political and financial shambles, and his people had been forced into indentured servitude under the Common Market, the European Union and the pressures of international trade. Germany was self-sufficient—at least the Germany Schleyer envisioned. A completely independent country, with plenty of land and money and the means to spread out far and wide. His was a country of joy and prosperity, a place other countries looked upon with respect and admiration.

Instead, the Americans had destroyed his land and his people, and Edel Schleyer was incensed at that thought. Nevertheless, he would pay them back. It would not be much longer until the project was complete. Then his bird of vengeance would fly. One would be sufficient for the moment, but later, he would amass an entire fleet of the new fighters.

America was going to pay.

Schleyer had never known hard times or poverty. He had been educated in the finest schools in the world and brought up in a home of bureaucratic power. Power. It was his single greatest aspiration. One day he would wield ultimate power, but at the moment he was content to stay the leading power of his country. Moreover, he could not go wrong with Linger's forces behind him. Schleyer had to hand it to Linger. His military force was certainly efficient, and the Iron Skull had proved its dedication time and again over the past year.

The forces Linger had assigned to guard Schleyer's fortress were impressive indeed. They rotated in three shifts, twelve hours guarding, twelve hours training and twelve hours of rest. The castle basement had become a barracks, and another large section had been devoted to assault training. The men also performed day and night maneuvers, setting their armored personnel carriers and all-terrain Hummers mounted with machine guns in tactical positions. Schleyer could make out guards roving along the top walls of the castle, their eyes probing the darkness, ready to respond to any threat with firepower and cunning.

They were worth every penny Schleyer paid them.

Eventually, he would approach Linger with his plans for storming the American Embassy in Berlin. Until then, they would proceed with the mission as planned. The key to success was to use cover, concealment and the elements of surprise—so Linger had told him. Schleyer was no military tactician and had never professed to being one. He was a businessman, and as German as any man he knew.

Schleyer turned and began to descend the circular stone stairwell leading to the central square. Most of the original decor had been left in place. Large banners hung from the walls, decorated with family or governmental emblems of the many dignitaries who had visited the castle throughout the centuries.

Schleyer had ordered some elements reinforced or repaired, but the castle was mostly in its original form. He had toyed with the idea of encircling the castle with a moat, but there was something too English in that thought. He had instead opted for barbed wire, an intruder system and remote-powered machine guns.

A truly deserving and proper home for a god, Schleyer thought.

As he continued down the steps, he considered the situation with Krizova. When the fighter was delivered and had been properly tested, Krizova and his daughter would have to die, of course. He was a bit puzzled at the Czech scientist's trusting nature. The man had served his government, a varying entity of political strife and internal chaos if there had ever been one, only to finally sell his secrets to the highest bidder.

Krizova had scoffed at Schleyer's original and more than generous offer. The German could have provided for Krizova and his daughter quite nicely. They would have had the best of protection, the finest of everything money could buy and unlimited technological resources. Instead, Krizova had sneered at Schleyer, mocking the offer and insinuating his distaste at dealing with somebody of Schleyer's background. It had been a fatal mistake, for both the Japanese and the Americans.

That would teach them to oppose his cause.

He reached the ground floor and pushed aside the wood-and-iron door. Another jaunt through a small chamber led him to the courtyard. Schleyer had ordered the roof removed from that portion of the castle, once again exposing the courtyard to the outside as it had been in its original design. In the center of the courtyard was a huge fountain, a gargoyle poised amid the quiet jet sprayers, like a demon bird ready to strike its unsuspecting prey. Shadows brought an almost lifelike appearance to the stone statue, cast by ornately carved bowls lit by built-in flood lamps.

At Schleyer's insistence, the castle was lit almost entirely with torches. Electricity had been installed on the perimeter defenses, to power cameras and other electronic gear, and the basement barracks were wired, as well. Schleyer felt torch lighting gave his home that medieval feeling, taking its occupants back to a time of knightly bravery and mysterious magic. After all, a god of mystery and medieval power would surround himself with a similar environment, one in which he was comfortable.

Schleyer slid his hands into the pockets of his tailored slacks and studied the gargoyle statue. It symbolized his euphoria and sense of immortality. He brushed casually at his graying hair before turning to head for the holding tower. He considered himself in the best shape of his life. He felt like twenty, rather than his actual fifty years of age, and he stuck to a three day per week aerobic-exercise regimen. As a result, he hardly felt winded as he hurried up the circular stairwell, which ended at a landing with a single door. An armed guard came to attention, snapping a smart salute, but Schleyer only nodded toward the door. The guard immediately whirled, inserting a key into the lock, then pushed the door open and stepped aside to allow Schleyer to pass.

Schleyer stepped through the doorway, and the guard closed and locked the door behind him. He smiled, an evil grin that sent a shudder through the woman chained to a wrought-iron bed. She was sitting atop a thin, dirty mattress, and the unmistakable chattering of rats echoed within the tower. The rats wouldn't venture close to the lovely woman, though—her delicate hand stroked a calico cat sleeping soundly in her lap.

Mila Krizova was quite beautiful, a young woman of barely eighteen, who had not lost any of her vibrancy or wide-eyed innocence. For the moment, Schleyer fully intended to make sure she stayed that way. Each applicant assigned to guard her had been personally interviewed by him before being allowed near the woman. Being cooped up in some castle fortress with a bunch of fellow soldiers for months at a time, without any form of recreation, could get to some men. Schleyer couldn't afford to let anything happen to Krizova's daughter at that point.

But later...

The young woman's eyes were almost black, even darker than Schleyer's, and they burned with hatred as she stared back at him. Her lip quivered, and her body trembled, the fear obvious in her near perfect features. She was still wearing the dress she'd had on at the time of her kidnapping, now torn and filthy. She had not been allowed to bathe. The food they gave her was enough to sustain her, and it was laced with a mild sedative, as well as powdered vitamins. It would not do to have her malnourished or dehydrated. Her feet were manacled to the bed, which in turn was welded to the floor, but she had enough length to use the stainless-steel toilet and sink installed into one wall.

"Well, my dear," Schleyer said, his cultured voice echoing in the confines of the tower, "I trust you are doing well?"

Krizova remained silent.

"Good, I am glad you are pleased with your accommodations."

He walked over to her and ran his hand down the side of her face, a sudden stirring in his groin. She was indeed beautiful, almost worthy to be a goddess. Schleyer fought back the urge to force himself upon her, opting to enjoy this game of intimidation. There was no challenge in raping a woman who was chained. Schleyer admired the kind of women who were beautiful, knew it and played hard-to-get because of that fact.

Krizova snapped her chin away from his touch, averting her eyes. "Don't touch me, you sick bastard." She spit on his hand.

Schleyer pulled his hand away, wiping it on the stained bedsheet. He shook his head sadly, then grabbed the motionless cat from her lap before she could stop him. He began to stroke the animal's head as he spoke softly to it. The cat mewed a protest, but Schleyer's surprisingly gentle touch and cradling warmth quickly placated the animal. Within moments, it was purring and relaxed again as Schleyer began to pace the room.

"You should learn some manners, my dear," Schleyer lectured. "Didn't your father ever teach you to respect your elders? Especially when they double as your intellectual superiors. I am quite surprised you would be so rude. You could learn a lot from me. I have been your host and treated you well. Yet you choose to repay that hospitality with curses and a generally poor attitude."

"You call taking me from my home and threatening me an act of hospitality?"

Schleyer stopped his pacing for a moment to face her with a harsh stare. "Do not take that tone with me, you insolent witch!" He lowered his voice and began to pace again before continuing his ruminations. "You should be grateful I have not simply ordered Commander Linger to slit your father's throat. He has been cooperative only because I have chosen to keep you alive. When the job is complete, I should think you will be reunited, and quite free to go your way. The fighter is all I want. I couldn't care less about you and your fool father."

"You're a liar."

Schleyer could see her eyes fixed on the cat in his arms, and she bit back any additional comments. So the animal was important to her. That was understandable, as it was the only contact with life she had for hours at a time, other than Schleyer's irregular visits. He would sometimes come in the night and simply stare at her as she slept. He wanted her, but it was not as much a sexual desire as simply the desire to impose his will on the weaker of the human species.

The cat lifted its head as Schleyer's strokes became more forceful.

"Why are you trying to resist me, my dear? You are pushing me to the limits of my patience."

"I know what you really want, and you are a sick monster. Do you think I am not aware of you coming here and watching me?"

Schleyer stopped his pacing to stare at her again. The smile that played across her lips was cold and dispassionate. She was laughing at him. She had scorned him and used him to find a way to get under his skin. She was a traitorous whore, unworthy of his attentions. There was only one thing to do.

"You will never see my vision," he said. "And for that, I cannot forgive you."

Krizova heard the snapping of bone before she lowered her eyes to see him wrench the cat's neck. There was only the briefest squeal from the animal. Its head fell limp on its broken neck, and Schleyer heaved the doll-like form directly at the young woman.

He turned and walked to the door as Krizova began to scream at him through a torrent of tears and gasping sobs. The guard immediately opened the door, and Schleyer smiled as the echoes of her screams followed him down the stairs.

As he pushed through the door on the ground level, he nearly ran into a short, voluptuous woman with fiery auburn hair, silky and cut to shoulder length. The woman's eyes were a deep green, and she had a heart-shaped face. She was quite sensual, standing there in her skintight leather pants and white silk blouse. A traditional fur wrap encircled her neck, and diamond studs glittered at her ears.

Schleyer felt that stirring in his groin again. Now, here was a true woman.

Gabrielle Reinmaul was a former BND agent with an

unusual talent for seduction. She was closer to Schleyer than any other person he'd associated with—she had served many years as his sort of alter ego. Schleyer didn't value just her advice. He valued her total surrender of body and mind to him. She was totally loyal to him and to his Germany of tomorrow.

"Gabrielle, what a pleasant surprise. When did you arrive?"

"Just now," she purred. Her eyes narrowed suspiciously. "Were you up there entertaining that Czech bitch?"

"She angered me, and I punished her."

"Wonderful," Reinmaul replied, tossing him a seductive smile. "She is not worthy of you, Edel." The woman slid her arms around Schleyer's neck and kissed him, probing his mouth and sharing the sweet taste of her tongue. "I, on the other hand, am everything you need."

Schleyer smiled, running his hands over Reinmaul's back and buttocks as a shudder of anticipation ran down his spine. He pushed thoughts of Mila Krizova from his mind, choosing to focus his attentions on the undoubtedly pleasurable tasks ahead. Gabrielle was almost a goddess—she was at least a godly tool for Schleyer to use and manipulate at will.

The thought of that aroused him.

3

"Lady," Mack Bolan growled, "you obviously have much more to lose than I do."

The Executioner smiled behind his pistol, although his ice-blue eyes lacked any warmth. They hadn't moved from their respective positions, guns trained on each other, each looking for an opening that gave an advantage. Still, it was the woman's move, and they both knew it.

In the taut silence that followed, her brown eyes softened slightly, and the earlier determination left her expression.

Bolan slowly lowered the Beretta only after the woman had holstered her Heckler & Koch HK4 pistol. He rose from his spot and attempted to assist her, as well, but she ignored his outstretched hand and jumped to her feet. He closed the apartment door as the woman shouldered past him and into the main living area, forcing herself not to look directly at him.

The soldier turned and was surprised to find a man lying sprawled in the middle of floor, a pool of congealed blood around his head. He matched the description of Bolan's contact, with his closely cropped brown hair and stocky frame. Parts of his slacks and shirt were splattered with dried blood, as well, and he wore a shoulder holster. A SIG P-220 pistol was near his outstretched hand.

"I assume that was my contact," Bolan said.

The woman sat on a couch opposite the body, separated from it by a low coffee table, and lit a cigarette from a pack on the table. She inhaled deeply, her hands shaking slightly, then blew out the smoke in a short gust. Her gaze finally went to Bolan, who stared expectantly at her.

"You killed him?"

"You would be correct," she shot back.

"I hope to hell you had a good reason for it," Bolan replied, holstering his Beretta. "Otherwise, we're not going to start off on the right foot."

"Don't threaten me, Mr. Belasko," she snapped.

Bolan tried to conceal his surprise, but he knew immediately she wasn't fooled. The woman might not have been experienced, but she was as sharp as a tack, and Bolan would have to be on his guard. The whole thing had already gone much farther than he'd originally anticipated.

"Would you mind telling me who you are?" Bolan nodded toward the body, adding, "And why you killed a CIA agent."

"My name is Jütta Kaufmann," she said, stubbing out her cigarette, her chin rising. "I am an agent for the Bundesnachrichtendienstes."

"The BND." Bolan nodded. "I know it well."

"You should, considering that you are thought to be an enemy to my country."

"Agent Kaufmann, I don't worry about everyone who considers me an enemy."

"Fair enough," she conceded. "But right now, I need you more to help me complete my mission than my government needs you in one of our prisons."

"What about my contact?"

"He was a double agent," she announced, shaking her head. "A traitor, like so many of his kind."

"I'd like to hear more about that," Bolan said, changing tack. "Right now, we're better off getting out of here. My hotel room is probably a little more secure."

Kaufmann smiled at his remark. "Is that an offer?"

"Hardly. Let's move."

Bolan followed her out, killing the lights and securing the apartment door behind him. He would need to contact CIA headquarters later, but now there were matters of greater importance.

Jütta Kaufmann was beautiful, but she was also dangerous. Her reactions hadn't been those of a hardened professional, but Bolan couldn't take chances. After the attempted hit at the airport, he wasn't about to let himself be taken by surprise again. The longer he exposed himself in unfamiliar territory, the more deadly the game got. It was a distinct possibility either one of them could have been followed to the apartment.

They walked briskly, covering the several blocks back to the hotel in only fifteen minutes. As they approached the intersection, Bolan grabbed the agent's hand and slowed his pace. The first step would be to check in with Stony Man. Any more information they could provide might point him in the right direction. Once he had direction, it was just a matter of tackling whoever held the ball.

Four hardmen suddenly emerged from a black Hummer parked across the street and a half block down. One of them who emerged stood out as the leader. He was tall and athletic, armed with only a pistol, and he barked something at his men as he waved in Bolan's direction. The Executioner turned toward the hotel and noticed two more men emerging from the lobby doors. Right at that moment, Bolan was glad he had remembered to take extra clips along for the ride.

He was going to need them.

A quick look revealed his left flank was open, the exit showing itself in the form of a stairwell leading to the U-Bahn platform below the city streets.

"Move!" he ordered, pushing Kaufmann toward the stairs while drawing the Beretta in a single smooth motion.

The two men from the hotel were closer, and they moved with the same precision as the group Bolan had encountered at the airport. They were obviously friends of the late opposition, and not the least bit shy about starting a firefight in the open. They rushed across the busy street, their Uzi machine pistols in plain view as they raced toward their target's position.

Bolan thumbed the safety, tracking on the closer gunman as he made a beeline for the stairwell. He squeezed the trigger, taking the gunner high and to the right, the slug boring through the man's shoulder. He spun into his teammate, causing temporary chaos in the middle of the street amid a cacophony of screaming drivers and blaring horns.

Bolan and Kaufmann descended the stairs and raced toward the platform. Luck or some unknown deity was with them, as a train approached from the distant darkness. The soldier ordered Kaufmann to follow him across the tracks, and the two leaped from the platform, crossing the pit in seconds. When Bolan turned to see a lone pursuer reach the bottom of the steps, he crouched to one knee, tracking on the man with a two-handed grip while motioning for Kaufmann to continue on. She used his upright knee as a foot stool, launching herself onto the platform.

Bolan thumbed the fire selector switch to 3-round bursts and triggered his pistol, hoping to keep the man's head down more than actually hit him. Fate smiled twice on the Executioner as his rounds found their target. The second burst blew holes in the gunman's head and chest, smearing the back wall with blood and brain matter.

Bolan suddenly remembered the approaching train as its horn blared and metal tires screeched against the tracks. He vaulted onto the platform, the train barely missing his legs as it passed. The soldier rolled away from the danger and got to his feet, rushing to where Kaufmann stood waiting.

The train passed quickly, and the remaining complement

of men arrived on the platform. They began to cross the tracks, firing on the run. Bolan crouched, yanking the German agent with him as gunfire raked the tiles around them, scarring the smooth surface and sending chips in every direction.

Kaufmann looked wildly in all directions, obvious panic in her eyes. Bolan had resigned himself to making a stand right there. Before he could return fire, the woman grabbed his shoulder and pointed in the direction of an obscure door in the corner of the platform. Bolan pulled her along with him as he headed for the door.

They reached the access door, and a well-placed shot from the Beretta took out the lock. The soldier pushed his companion across the threshold door, firing another burst at the advancing enemy before following her. He could hear rounds striking the iron doorway as he popped his spent magazine and slammed a fresh one home.

The tunnel was long, narrow and poorly lit. It was lined with utility pipes along the walls, and bare bulbs hung above at lengthy intervals. Bolan considered the odds as Kaufmann led them through the passageway. There was no place to hide, and a standoff against four men armed with machine pistols wasn't a viable option in a place without sufficient cover.

The enemy could hardly miss in such narrow confines.

The German agent stopped suddenly.

"What's the problem?" he demanded.

She only smiled, pointing straight up. Bolan's eyes followed her finger to the bottom rung of a ladder protruding from a circular ladder well.

"It leads up to the street," she said triumphantly.

"Go," he replied, bending down and cupping his hands.

Kaufmann stepped into his grip, and he hurled her up to the well. She snagged the lower rung, pulling herself up without considerable effort, followed by Bolan. They climbed the ladder quickly, and the soldier could make out the shouts of surprise. The gunmen were obviously perplexed. They wouldn't be able to see the ladder from the doorway, so it would appear as if their prey had simply vanished.

Moments later, they pushed through the manhole cover and were back in the deserted square, now a half block from the hotel. It was obvious they couldn't go back there, so neither of them even bothered to suggest it. They turned and began to walk away.

As they entered the neighboring district, they were suddenly surrounded by darkened stores. It was a major shopping district, the walkways deserted except for an occasional couple and a few drunks using the window displays to keep themselves upright. They had walked several blocks when Bolan's combat instincts flared.

It was too quiet.

He proceeded another block before grabbing Kaufmann's arm and steering her into a narrow alley. She began to protest, but he cut her off with a finger to his lips, and pulled her close before whispering in her ear.

"We're being followed. Stand right here, and whatever you do, don't look in my direction."

Bolan ducked into the shadows of a large brick building. He didn't have long to wait, as the tall athletic man they had first spotted by the Hummer appeared around the corner, his movements furtive. The man stopped short and stared at the innocent shadow of Kaufmann's outline against the distant streetlights. A smile played across Niktor Hess's lips a moment before he heard Bolan.

Wraithlike, the Executioner stepped from the shadows of the building and grabbed the man. Hess moved with unexpected speed, drawing a knife from seemingly nowhere. He slashed at Bolan's outstretched arm, and the soldier grunted, gritting his teeth against the pain as the sharp blade ripped through his jacket and bit into the flesh beneath.

Bolan crouched slightly, maintaining a low center of balance, and waited patiently. Hess feinted to the left, but the soldier didn't fall for it. Hess's hurried attempt to follow up on the feint was his mistake. He lunged at his adversary's chest with the knife. Bolan stepped to the outside of the lunge, gripping the wrist of the knife hand with some effort, and smashed his forearm into his opponent's locked elbow joint. The man yelped in pain. Bolan snatched his opponent's collar and yanked him in a backward, twisting motion while driving his knee into the small of the guy's back.

The move was effective, snapping the spine like a twig. The scream of pain died before Bolan let his attacker drop to the ground in a crumpled heap. Ragged breaths escaped from the unconscious man's throat, and if he didn't die from the shock to his spinal cord, he would most likely suffer permanent paralysis.

Kaufmann rushed to look at Bolan's arm.

"We need to get you some medical attention."

"No doctors," Bolan countered. "My car's not far from here. Just get me someplace safe, and a medical kit. I can tend to my own wounds."

"Come on."

They began to make their way down the alley.

JÜTTA KAUFMANN'S apartment was a cramped, one-bedroom walk-up located in a district on the outskirts of Frankfurt. Griesheim was predominantly residential, and the nondescript four-story structure stood in the very center of the district. It was solid, with a brick exterior, and the interior wasn't much more impressive. The furnishings inside the apartment were simple, and the decor hardly elegant. The apartment was actually comprised of three rooms, a bedroom, a living area and a kitchen that doubled as a bath-room. There was no toilet, just a shower stall. The building had a community toilet on the second floor, so cleaning up in there had been out of the question.

The wound in Bolan's arm was deep, but Kaufmann was quite skilled. Her BND survival training paid off. She cleaned, disinfected and sutured the wound within fifteen minutes. The work was swift and efficient, as good as any medical doctor could have done. Her first-aid kit also contained antibiotics and a tetanus booster.

After putting on some coffee, the woman sat at the kitchen table and lit a cigarette. She watched Bolan intently as he quickly dressed the wound in sterile gauze and a roller bandage. Once he finished, he borrowed her pistol, tucking it in his waistband before field-stripping the Beretta 93-R.

"Do you have any shaving cream?" he asked her.

The woman nodded, rising from the table and returning a few moments later with a can of shaving cream. Bolan quickly doused the moving parts of his autopistol with it, then set the weapon carefully on some discarded newspaper before noting Kaufmann's perplexed expression.

"I have never seen this before," she finally said.

"What?"

"Cleaning a gun in such a manner."

"The properties in shaving cream draw the gunpowder and metal fouling from the weapon," Bolan explained.

"Most interesting." She smiled, inhaling deeply on her cigarette before adding, "I will have to remember that."

Kaufmann slapped her forehead and offered the cigarette pack to Bolan. He gave a quick shake of his head, and she returned the pack to the table. She then turned in her chair to face him directly.

"You don't believe me, do you?" she asked, nodding to her weapon.

"You mean about my contact being a traitor?"

She nodded curtly.

Bolan shrugged. "I don't know you, and I have no reason to trust you. Especially since you haven't told me what you were doing in his apartment."

"That is hardly of consequence," the agent said with a dismissive wave. "I killed him in self-defense. As far as trusting me, I could have killed you, too, but instead I tried to take you alive. That should count for something."

"In this business, it doesn't count for anything," Bolan said.

"You will never be convinced, will you?"

"I've listened so far, haven't I?" he said, leaning back and crossing his arms.

Kaufmann let out an exhausted sigh before speaking. "Several years ago, shortly after my appointment to the service, I was assigned to track down a man named Dortmund Linger. He was a commander with the BND before the cold war ended, and an exceptionally talented agent on top of that. After his deactivation, the service offered him a desk position. He turned it down, and his answer came in the way of murder. Twenty-six people were killed, all key personnel within the service. Every one of them found was with their throats slit."

An eerie feeling washed over Bolan upon hearing that last. The Japanese businessmen found murdered in the Czech Republic had all died the same way.

"Go on," Bolan said.

"Commander Linger is a very dangerous man, and recent intelligence reports have led us to believe he now has a private army. We do not know who is financing them, but we know they are out there. I suspect the men who attacked us tonight did so under his orders. He is well-connected in both the German community and abroad. I will not bother you with the details of what atrocities I have seen this man commit. Let me simply say I have been tracking him for many years now, and he is very elusive. I got closer than ever tonight, after discovering your contact was there looking for the same thing I was.''

''What was that?''

''Information on another CIA operative named Carter Wiley. Actually, the apartment is an old safehouse Wiley used. Nobody else supposedly knew about it. At least, nobody other than Wiley's superiors.''

''Why are you interested in Wiley?''

''Because he was supposed to provide me a solid lead on Linger. I also found out your contact was there for another purpose.''

''Which was?'' Bolan prodded.

Kaufmann fixed him with a hard look before rising and pouring their coffee. ''To kill you,'' she replied nonchalantly, setting the coffee in front of him before taking her seat again.

It was all beginning to make sense now.

Wiley had been assigned by his office to arrange the meet between the Japanese and Krizova. Afterward, he was supposed to get Krizova and his daughter back to Frankfurt and see them off on a direct flight to the States. Instead, the Japanese were killed, and Wiley and the Krizovas were missing. The connection with this Dortmund Linger was overwhelming. Bolan was convinced Linger had something to do with the meet going sour. It was too important to be tossed away as mere coincidence, and Bolan had never been a real believer in such things anyway.

Besides the fact, he had no other leads at that point.

The answers were probably still locked away somewhere inside Carter Wiley's apartment, and Bolan intended to find them.

DORTMUND LINGER had not been looking forward to meeting with Edel Schleyer. The man made him nervous. He wasn't worried about reporting their failure to bring down the mysterious American. Schleyer usually couldn't be bothered with such details. Linger had been hired to take care of problems like these, and he would only mention it as a courtesy.

Linger's nervousness stemmed more from having to tell Schleyer the project could be pushed back because of their new adversary. Linger had also recognized the woman outside the American's hotel. She was BND, and she had been following his trail for many years. At first, Linger had considered her only a minor annoyance. Now the bitch had allied herself with the American agent. Linger had studied the man's moves, and he knew the stranger wasn't a novice. Grubel had been correct in his assessment—the man was definitely a soldier.

"We might have a problem," Linger announced.

They were sitting in Schleyer's makeshift office at the fortress, and the man seemed determined to finish the bottle of whiskey brought to them by one of several servants Schleyer kept on hand. They sat at a small table that was decorated with white linen. Schleyer was downing a tumbler of the iced whiskey between bites of baked pork sausage and helpings of potato pancakes.

Linger had barely touched his food.

"What kind of problem?" Schleyer mumbled around a mouthful of sausage.

"Nothing serious. That American I told you about, the one sent by the CIA. He took out an entire unit of men, and another six of some of my very best near his hotel." Linger paused before adding, "I also watched him kill my executive officer with his bare hands. Captain Hess was a seasoned combat veteran."

Schleyer nearly gagged on his food. He excused himself, setting down his utensils and dabbing at his mouth. He didn't say anything for a long moment.

"It sounds serious to me," Schleyer remarked. "What do you make of that?"

"He is a professional soldier," Linger replied with a casual shrug. "There is no question we are dealing with more than just a CIA agent. No, this man is very special."

"You are saying the CIA did not send him?"

"I am not certain about that, although my instinct tells me no."

Schleyer was silent for a time, and Linger waited for him to collect his thoughts. He knew the man's highly educated mind was probing for answers, feeling out the situation. There was an unquestionable spark of hesitancy in Schleyer's eyes, and Linger smelled trouble. Indecision bred sloppiness, and the mercenary didn't have time to wait for Schleyer to come up with some answers. He knew how to handle the situation, but he wasn't about to show his hand yet. If he told Schleyer he wanted to pull some men from the project too quickly, he knew the man would resist the idea totally.

"What are you proposing to do about this?"

"We could set up an ambush."

"It sounds as if that tactic hasn't worked thus far," Schleyer countered sarcastically.

"I wasn't speaking of a direct attack," Linger said. "Sometimes these things require a more indirect touch."

"What do you mean?"

"There was a woman with him, a BND agent named Jütta Kaufmann. She was assigned to find me several years ago, but I have managed to elude her up to this point. This last incident put her closer than ever, and she has become a thorn in my side, one I now find myself compelled to deal with." Linger's voice had taken a chilling edge.

Schleyer blinked. "Why didn't you tell me about this before?"

"Because it had nothing to do with our plans. It still

doesn't. My point is, sometimes a threat is best dealt with by applying pressure to an outside source, rather than to the central object."

"I see," Schleyer interjected. "You think by threatening this Kaufmann, you can lure the true target into the snare."

"Why not? We can't know for certain until we have tried, and this has the double advantage of finally getting rid of this woman. I can do away with her as quietly as I did Wiley."

"What happens if this man doesn't respond as you believe he will?" Schleyer asked, as if he'd been reading Linger's mind. "What then?"

"I have taken that into account, but I am certain he will. If necessary, I will deal with that issue when it arises."

Schleyer fell silent again, and Linger let him dwell on the proposition. So far, Schleyer hadn't asked about the effects of such a plan on the project. He wasn't an idiot, though, and he surely knew the consequences of failure. A little prevention would go a long way to keeping the project on schedule, and if the timetable did become unbalanced, it wouldn't take long to recover the momentary lapse in manpower. Linger had to convince Schleyer of this fact.

Linger wasn't about to commit large forces in finding and eliminating one man. Such things were foolish. It would take only a few men, and he didn't even plan to bring it up, if it was at all possible. Kaufmann wouldn't be a problem. Once he had made the threat obvious, the American would come running to her rescue—Linger was convinced of that.

"I don't like it," Schleyer finally replied. "So far, your men have failed to bring him down. Obviously, this man has no idea of our plans. Therefore, I don't propose him to be an immediate threat. I think our mistake has been to take the fight to him, instead of letting him come to us. Furthermore, I don't want anything standing in the way of completing the fighter on time.'' Schleyer shook his head. ''No, I can't allow you to proceed on this, Commander Linger. For now, we will continue as planned, and I want to accelerate our efforts.''

Linger wanted to strangle Schleyer, but he refused to let his emotions get the better of him. He clenched his fists under the table, biting back the impulse to argue his point. Schleyer was oblivious to Linger, returning to the food with his original tenacity.

''What if I was to pursue this on my own?'' Linger ventured.

''I need you to stay on top of the good doctor,'' Schleyer retorted. ''As for this woman agent with the BND... What was her name?''

''Kaufmann.''

''Yes. I will put Gabi on that. She is perfectly suited for such a job.''

''As you wish, sir,'' Linger muttered.

If Schleyer heard the loathing in Linger's voice, he made no sign of it.

Mack Bolan was a motionless silhouette as he crouched on the rooftop of a building across from Carter Wiley's apartment. An economy sedan was parked near the front of the building, with four men seated inside. Lookouts.

Bolan checked his watch. He was running out of time. He had been up and moving well before dawn, and leaving Kaufmann sleeping soundly at her apartment. She would be angry with him, but he had to stick by his policy of working alone. The woman had guts and brains, and he didn't wish to see either of them spilled. It would only be more innocent blood on his hands. She might be a good BND agent, but the scales had tipped in the enemy's favor.

The information Kaufmann had given him was enough to go on for the moment. Intel regarding Krizova's disappearance could be at Carter Wiley's apartment. Bolan hated to betray Kaufmann's trust, but he considered his mission more important. The security of a few people was at stake while this Linger was at large, but Bolan's objectives were on a grander scale. If an enemy force, particularly terrorists, *did* have something to do with the kidnapping of Vasec Krizova, the lives of millions of people could be at stake.

Bolan had parked the Citroën a few blocks away, changing into his blacksuit in the vehicle. The Beretta 93-R was holstered in its customary place under his left arm, and the soldier was girded for war with his combat harness over the blacksuit. Black camouflage paint was smeared across his face and hands, and the Desert Eagle hung at his right hip. The HK53 was within reach, propped against the knee-high wall surrounding the edge of the rooftop, and Bolan's sniper rifle was set up on its bipod, wedged between a crumbling break in the wall.

The Executioner had expected the enemy to be watching the apartment. He would have preferred a soft probe, but with his opposition close, he knew there was no way to get inside the apartment undetected. He wasn't even sure what he was looking for. Kaufmann had mentioned Wiley had information, and Bolan's instincts told him it was probably hidden inside the apartment in some form or another.

First, he needed to deal with the opposition.

Bolan leaned down to peer through the infrared scope of the sniper rifle. The rifle was a recent addition to Bolan's arsenal. John "Cowboy" Kissinger had first been attracted to the weapon while attending a U.S. Army weapons demonstration. It was a GIAT FR-F2, a precision bolt-action rifle of French design. Based on the old MAS36 service rifle, the weapon had a thermal insulating sleeve over the barrel to reduce the infrared signature. The magazine capacity was ten rounds, and the weapon chambered 7.62 mm cartridges.

The driver's left chest filled the scope, and Bolan adjusted the focus slightly to align the crosshairs on his target. Taking out the driver would serve to immobilize the vehicle, and the soldier was counting on the element of surprise. The men had been assigned to what they most likely considered boring duty. Bolan was about to give them more action then they had anticipated.

Bolan took a deep breath, let half out, and waited a second before squeezing the trigger. The rifle cracked as the round left the barrel with an exit velocity of over 600 meters per second. The bullet contacted the target in less than a second, punching a clean hole through the window and into the man's chest, continuing through until it lodged in the seat cushion behind him.

At the moment of impact, Bolan yanked the bolt to the rear and slammed a fresh round home. He sighted into the back seat, movement inside the vehicle visible through the scope as its occupants scrambled to get clear. The two men on the passenger's side would have been safer if they had remained inside the vehicle, but the explosion of blood and torn tissue from the chest of their comrade created the panic on which Bolan had counted.

The gunman seated behind the driver flung his door open and attempted to bail out. It was the last mistake he ever made as Bolan led him in the scope. The Executioner's second shot scored a direct hit, slamming between the gunman's shoulders, tossing him a considerable distance before he hit the ground. His body twitched slightly, then became still.

The two men on the passenger's side were now clear of the vehicle as Bolan chambered a third round. One of them remained behind the car, while the other sought cover in a narrow span between two nearby apartment buildings. Dogs began to bark, and panicked voices could be heard coming from a few scattered apartments, lights coming on behind curtained windows.

Bolan was up and moving across the rooftop for a better vantage point, taking the HK53 with him. The gunman behind the vehicle rose from his position, a Steyr MPi81 clutched in his hands. The weapon chattered, spitting rounds at Bolan at a cyclic rate of 700 rounds per minute. Nine millimeter Parabellum rounds gouged into the masonry wall, trailing behind Bolan as he ran. He leaped to the next rooftop, landing in a shoulder roll and coming to his feet with catlike grace.

The soldier swung the HK53 into play and loosed a hail of rounds at the enemy. Several slugs scored the roof of the sedan, coring through or ricocheting off its slick. One of the 5.56 mm NATO rounds buried itself in the gunman's arm. The bullet struck a nerve, numbing the man's arm and causing him to lose control of his weapon. He slumped to the ground in shock, his Steyr clattering to the pavement out of reach.

Bolan continued his course to the end of the rooftop. He peered over the side, staring at the hard ground far below—no exit that way. He hurried to the rear, moving out of sight of his opponents. Spying a fire-escape ladder, the soldier quickly descended. He vaulted the privacy fence surrounding the building courtyard and made his way along the side of the building until he reached the street. He crouched at the edge of the building and peered around the corner.

The gunman behind the car was no longer visible, but Bolan had a perfect view of the man crouched between the apartment buildings. He stared upward, his attention drawn to the rooftops, waiting for Bolan to show himself again. The Executioner stepped into the open and sprinted across the street, keeping his weapon on the man. The gunman noticed the movement and fired his Uzi, squeezing the trigger before he made target acquisition.

Bolan returned fire, the rounds from the HK53 slamming the gunner against one of the building's walls. He collapsed to the ground in a lifeless heap.

Bolan managed to reach the back of the sedan before the remaining gunman could scramble to his weapon. The soldier stomped on the man's outstretched fingers, pointing the hot barrel of the HK53 between the gunman's eyes. The man said nothing, pressing his lips tightly together.

"You speak English?" Bolan asked.

The shouting of neighbors had died down, and Bolan could hear the sirens in the distance. He didn't have much time, so he raised the weapon.

"I guess not," Bolan stated.

"W-wait," the terrorist said, "I sp-speak English well."

"Then you have a few seconds to tell me who you are, and why I shouldn't kill you right here."

"Please, don't shoot," the man protested, gesturing to Bolan with his free hand. "I am just a common man. I work to feed my family…that's all."

"Your time is about up," Bolan said, shaking his head. "Talk quick!"

"I know only that I work for a big blond man. A German. It was him who ordered us to watch this place."

"Where do I find this guy?"

"I do not know. He hired me and my friends only to keep an eye out for you. It was all arranged by that man you just killed." He waved in the direction of the dead man between the apartments. "I heard him talk about somebody named Schleyer. A wealthy man. That is all I know."

The name didn't ring any bells for Bolan. With time, he probably could have coerced more information from the man. However, time wasn't a luxury the Executioner had—it was time to go, and he couldn't risk being seen. He rapped the butt of his weapon behind the man's ear, knocking him unconscious. These men hadn't been the professionals Bolan had dealt with before, and he wouldn't kill a man in cold blood. It was up to the German police to deal with him now.

Bolan quickly looked inside the vehicle before trotting to Wiley's apartment. He slipped inside under the cover of darkness. It would be a while before the police began to canvass the area for those who might have risked a look out their windows, and by that time he would be long gone.

The soldier quickly entered the apartment, slinging his HK53 before producing a miniflashlight from his combat harness. The window to the apartment was covered by a curtain, and the blue lights of the police squad cars flashed against them, giving the room the effect of a discotheque. The body of his CIA contact was still in place, and the room was beginning to smell. Bolan rifled through every drawer and cupboard, but after searching nearly a half hour, he still found nothing that brought him closer to the answers he sought.

As he descended the stairs and made his way out the back door of the apartment, he had become certain of only one thing. Someone had undoubtedly killed Carter Wiley and snatched Krizova. A terrorist group of some sort was probably holding the Czech scientist, but there had been no ransom demands. Krizova was too valuable to eliminate. That meant whoever was behind the whole thing could actually be forcing Krizova to build the jet fighter.

Bolan figured it was time to contact the CIA about their dead agent. He didn't intend to tell them about Jütta Kaufmann this early in the game. If she was right, he could no longer trust anybody at the CIA headquarters in Frankfurt. He would report the man's death as a matter of duty, and see if they had more information. As the Executioner stole away from the area, heading back toward his vehicle, he considered his probe hadn't been a total loss. He did have something—a name.

AFTER CLEANING UP by the Main River, then checking into a nearby waterfront motel, Bolan drove to the CIA headquarters in Frankfurt. The building was located in the center of the uptown area, surrounded by international hotels and businesses. It was single storied, painted a flat gray and looked very shabby nestled in among the other more corporate structures.

The Central Intelligence Agency's presence in Germany was nearly a contradiction in terms. The operation was hardly clandestine, and their ranks had been penetrated repeatedly by sleeper agents. The CIA was more of a clearinghouse for information on the German economy, and they had turned to catering to the needs of American officials or high-ranking members of the business world. Secrets were no longer valuable in a post-cold war era, unless those secrets made men powerful and wealthy.

When national security became an issue, the CIA was no more qualified to investigate it than the FBI or NSA. They couldn't legally operate within the confines of the U.S. The Treasury Department was generally assigned to protecting political officials traveling abroad, and the Marine Corps handled security for the embassies. This left the CIA out in the cold, with the espionage business having largely gone by the wayside.

Bolan wasn't sure how the Agency could help, but it was his only connection to Stony Man. Bolan parked his car and entered the building. The reception desk was unoccupied. It was possible the secretary was on an errand, but Bolan didn't have time to wait. He worked his way past the desk and down a small corridor. A door at the end read Dan Lincoln, Frankfurt Case Chief.

The door was partially open, and Bolan peered inside. The office was sparsely furnished, with a small window in the back wall. A miniature fan rested on the ledge in front of the window, groaning in protest as it fought to bring fresh air into the stuffy room. A cheap government desk stood in one corner, and a man sat in the chair behind it. His feet were propped up on the desk, and he was tossing darts at a corkboard with Saddam Hussein's likeness pasted on it.

He was a younger man, perhaps in his midthirties, dressed in tan slacks and vest over a cream-colored shirt. A dark brown tie was loosely knotted at his open collar, and his lips were pinched together in concentration as he tossed another dart at the corkboard. His face was clear, and his blue eyes sparkled in the fluorescent lights scattered throughout the low tile ceiling. He hadn't noticed Bolan yet, seemingly focused on the task of trying to get a bull's-eye.

"Excuse me," Bolan said sharply, rapping on the door.

The man turned a startled gaze in the soldier's direction. He took his feet off the desk, stood up and dropped the remaining darts in his hand on the desk. He was a bit younger than Bolan had originally guessed, and maybe a half foot shorter than the Executioner, with a slight paunch unusual for men his age.

"Can I help you, sir?" the man asked.

Bolan jerked a thumb at the nameplate on the door. "Are you Lincoln?"

"Yep, that's me. Who are you?"

"The name's Belasko," Bolan said, entering the room and offering his hand, "but you can call me Mike."

Lincoln took the stranger's hand uncertainly. "You're American."

"Uh, yeah," Bolan countered. "Is that surprising or something?"

"No, it's just that I don't get to talk to Americans very often," Lincoln said. He gestured toward a chair in front of his desk. "Other than my own agents, anyway. Are you with the Company?"

"Not exactly," Bolan said, tossing the man a wary smile. "As a matter of fact, I'm here to talk about one of your agents. I take it you don't recognize my name."

"No. Was I supposed to be expecting you?"

"Not really," Bolan replied. He looked around the room and added, "Are we secure here?"

Lincoln smiled, and Bolan's muscles became taut as the case chief reached into his top desk drawer. Instead of a weapon, Lincoln pulled out a short tube with a screen tip and a plastic handle. Bolan immediately recognized the bug-sweeping device.

"I go over the place three times a day. It's the most advanced one we've been able to get our hands on at present, but it does the trick. Besides, nobody comes in or out of here without my knowing about it. I try to keep the place as tight a drum, so you don't have to worry."

"Is that why I was just able to walk in here without anybody questioning me?"

Lincoln cleared his throat, staring hard at Bolan before putting the electronic gadget back in his drawer. He closed it with some force, but Bolan didn't even blink. He wasn't here to discuss security measures, but he was cautious of men like Lincoln. He might have just been young, inexperienced and cocky, but those were all things that could kill a person quickly. Bolan knew he couldn't be overly critical. It was important he contact Brognola, whether the liaison was a young, snot-nosed kid or an experienced veteran.

"Sorry," the soldier continued, "just grouchy, I guess. Jet lag, you know?"

"It's all right," Lincoln said good-naturedly.

"Listen, I don't have a lot of time, and I'm going to need your help. I was sent here by people you don't know to investigate the disappearance of the Krizovas and an agent named Carter Wiley. Was he one of your men?"

Something went flat in Lincoln's eyes at the mention of Wiley's name. "Yes. Carter was one of my best men. I've been very concerned about him, and it seems like it's taken forever for someone in Wonderland to get off their ass and give us some assistance with—"

Lincoln cut himself short and snapped his fingers. "Wait a minute! Are you who was supposed to meet our contact at Wiley's place?"

"Yeah," Bolan replied with a nod. "That's part of the

bad news I have for you. Your agent's dead. The apartment was unsecured, and somebody put a bullet in his head. Just before that, a group of men armed with automatic weapons tried to take me out at the airport shortly after I arrived, and then I was attacked again last night. I don't know what the hell is going on, but I'm figuring it's all related to whatever happened to Wiley and the Krizovas."

Breath exploded from Lincoln's lungs. "The meet with you was supposed to be routine. Okay, who's behind it?"

"I don't know, but I need you to get word back to Washington and bring them up to speed. I'm also going to need a different vehicle, some ammunition in 5.56 and 9 mm and any information you might have obtained to this point."

"Whoa—wait a minute here," Lincoln said, raising his hands. "Slow down a minute, pal. I can't just start forking out equipment and information without some kind of authorization."

Bolan whipped a card out of his jacket pocket and tossed it on Lincoln's desk. "Then call that number and get it."

"I can do that, but first I need to know more about what you've discovered."

"I haven't 'discovered' anything," Bolan said. "And every minute we sit here having a discussion group about how much neither of us knows, the more serious the situation becomes, and the less my chances of ever finding Dr. Krizova, his daughter or your own man. So call."

"I'll get in touch with them later," Lincoln said.

He reached inside his pocket and tossed a set of keys at Bolan. "In the meantime, you can use Carter's vehicle. It's an old maroon Dodge Aries parked up the street, but it runs."

As Lincoln reached into a lower desk drawer, Bolan's hand went to the butt of the Beretta under his jacket. "Easy," he cautioned.

Lincoln stared at Bolan a moment, then nodded and looked away, apparently searching the drawer hard before finally pulling out a thick manila folder. He opened it to verify the contents, then set it down on the desk and shoved it across to Bolan.

"There's everything I've got. Those are copies, so once you've gone through the information, destroy it."

"Thanks. I have just one other question. Does the name Schleyer ring any bells to you?"

Lincoln appeared to ponder the question for some time, and Bolan wasn't sure if the kid was really thinking on it, or knew the name and wasn't telling. In either case, something in his reaction didn't seem right. He was more convinced he would have to watch the young man. Bolan didn't like the way things had played out so far, and he was no longer sure of whom he could trust.

"No, I don't think so," Lincoln finally replied. "Although it's not an uncommon name in Germany, believe it or not. Where did you hear it?"

"Just picked it up somewhere. I don't even know if it has any importance."

"I can look into it if you'd like."

Bolan shrugged. "If you want, that's up to you."

"Fine," Lincoln replied with a cordial smile. "It will be a few hours before I can get you any ammunition or weapons. First, I'll have to contact your people in Washington and get their authorization."

"You'll get it," Bolan snapped.

"Where do I get in touch with—?"

"You don't," the soldier said, rising and tucking the folder inside his jacket. He looked at his watch. "I'll contact you by phone in four hours. We can set up a meet then."

"Okay."

As Bolan crossed the room and reached the door, Lincoln

called to him. "Do you really think there's a chance Wiley's still alive?"

"Slim," Bolan replied grimly.

AFTER BOLAN HAD LEFT the office, Dan Lincoln considered his situation. The guy was definitely not with the Company. That made him most likely NSA. His mission was important enough to get the attention of the President, so Lincoln wasn't about to try to cross the guy. Most puzzling was the fact the guy had mentioned Schleyer's name.

That definitely wasn't good. If the big man with the cold blue eyes was on to Schleyer, he was on to Linger. And if he was on to Linger, well...

Lincoln picked up the phone and dialed a local number, letting it ring for several moments. After some time passed with no answer, he hung up and dialed another number. This was the special line, the one he had been instructed to use only in emergencies. A fine, cultured voice answered on the second ring. Lincoln winced, because it sounded as if he had awakened the caller.

"It's me," Dan Lincoln announced.

"What is it?"

"We might have a problem."

"I have been hearing about a lot of those today. What is wrong?"

"That agent sent from the States just showed up in my office."

There was a silence. Then, "You promised me you would take care of that problem. This man is really becoming a thorn in my side. I want him eliminated."

"My man was supposed to wait for him," Lincoln countered, "but somebody beat him there. He says somebody killed the contact."

"Yes, and that individual is working with him."

"Who?"

"Some bitch with the BND. It doesn't really matter, because I already have someone on her. You need to concentrate on holding up your end of the bargain."

"That's going to be a little difficult with the guy snooping around here and dropping names."

"Where did he get names?"

"I don't know. Maybe you should ask your friends."

"Do not get smart with me, *schweinhund,* or you might be joining your American friends."

"Listen, I'm doing what I promised to do."

"And you are being well paid for it," the voice reminded him. "Do not forget who it is you work for."

"I'll remember," Lincoln snorted. "What about this Belasko guy?"

"Now listen to me. This is what I want you to do...."

5

Washington, D.C.

Hal Brognola sat on the park bench, reading the newspaper. He squinted in the dim light of the lamppost behind him, while chomping on an unlit cigar. As he waited impatiently for the President's arrival, he tried to concentrate on the stock exchange reports, but his attempts were futile. The only thing he could seem to think of was an old friend who might be in a lot of trouble.

An unmarked limousine suddenly appeared to his left, and Brognola muttered a sigh of relief. He stood, rolled the paper under his arm and marched dutifully across the brown, windswept lawn. The big Fed's feet crunched on the dry, fallen leaves as he walked, signaling that another winter was drawing near. He was really going to have to speak with the President about the longevity of this new procedure. The exposure would surely kill him, if he didn't die of old age first.

Brognola was quickly frisked by two Secret Service agents, then entered the limousine, grateful for the warmth of the interior. The thermostat of the President's limousine kept the vehicle a perfect seventy degrees at all time. It was a veritable sweat box when Brognola compared it to the outside air, but he didn't mind. Anything was better than that bitter wind.

"Good evening, Hal. How are you?" the President asked.

"A bit chilly, sir, but none the worse for wear," Brognola replied.

"Yes, I'm sorry about these measures. I know it's inconvenient, but I didn't feel secure discussing this matter at the White House. I hope you understand my position."

"Well enough, sir," Brognola replied, pulling off his gloves and unbuttoning his heavy wool overcoat.

"Has there been any other word?"

"No, there hasn't. I'm really quite relieved you called this meeting."

"Oh?" the President replied. He raised his eyebrows, adding, "Has something happened to your man?"

"We're not quite sure, Mr. President," Brognola began. "He's only twelve hours past check-in, but that's not the unusual part. I'm sure you're aware his schedule isn't necessarily the same as ours."

"Yes, Hal, I'm all too aware of that," the President said tightly. "What else can you tell me?"

"Without word from our inside man, I can't give you an update, sir. I think I know a way to remedy the situation, but I'm not completely sure you would like the idea."

"Try me. Maybe I'll surprise you."

Brognola could feel a warm glow ignite within him. The President wasn't always the easiest man to work for, but then the same had been true of his predecessors. This man was open-minded but strong willed, and the big Fed had already practiced the argument, running it through his mind several times to figure out the best way to present the case. He wanted to get right to the point, but the issue was a bit complicated.

"Mr. President, we need more information on this fighter. It's that simple. Striker doesn't know the first thing about the weapon, yet I've asked him to assess the risks, find out what happened to Dr. Krizova and take action based upon the results of his investigation. He has no backup support, and I have no way of contacting him, since you have insisted we rely only on communication through official channels. That's a tall order.''

"I know, Hal," the President interjected, "and I understand your frustrations, believe me. This is a very sensitive issue, though. I just can't risk the lives of countless people, or the national security of this country, without some kind of hard evidence. You knew that when you sent him in, and you know it now.''

"And I would concur with you, sir," Brognola rebutted, "if I thought this information was truly sensitive enough to warrant absolute secrecy. However, I can't promise results if you don't give me a little leeway now and then. We have three people missing, and five Japanese businessmen have been killed. One of those men was a personal friend of yours.''

The President nodded slowly in way of reply.

"I'm inclined to believe you don't want any more people to die," Brognola pressed, "regardless of their position in this. Sure, Striker knows the risks, but there's a lot more at stake here than the life of one man. We haven't heard anything from our CIA contacts, and that really bothers me. Furthermore, there are people within my organization who could come up with alternate plans of action if this one fails.

"The success of the mission hinges on three things," Brognola continued. He held up each finger as he listed them. "Locating the Krizovas, locating the fighter plans and getting both safely to the United States. We can't assess all of the potential threats with only half the information.''

"Give me an example.''

"How about whether or not somebody could find a way

to coerce Krizova into actually building this blasted thing. Worse yet, how about simply exploiting him for money?''

''There's been no ransom demand.''

''Not yet,'' Brognola countered. ''That's probably because we don't even know who we're dealing with. This could be an action by a foreign government, somebody from our own government, even a terrorist group.''

''That doesn't sound like their style,'' the President said.

''Maybe not, sir,'' Brognola replied, ''but wouldn't you feel more comfortable being prepared for every eventuality?''

There was a long silence before the President spoke again. ''What's the bottom line, Hal?''

''I need more to work with, sir. I need the information on that fighter so I can make some better decisions. I need the intelligence, and I'm asking you to trust me on this one.'' His voice softened some.

There was another long pause as the President appeared to think it over. Brognola could feel his palms sweating. Getting the technical information on the fighter would give them a better chance of finding Krizova. At least, they would have all the cards on the table, and they could devise an alternative form of action if Striker didn't come through. He hadn't lied to the President. He had simply given him the situation as it stood.

''All right, Hal,'' the President conceded, ''I'll give you everything we know on this. However, I want a complete list of all persons with access to the information, and they will not be allowed to leave the Farm without my personal okay. Is that fair enough?''

''Fair enough, sir,'' Brognola replied triumphantly. ''And thank you, Mr. President. Will that be all?''

''Not yet,'' the President said. ''We still have the reason I called this meeting to begin with.''

''Of course. What is it?''

"We received a communiqué from authorities in the upper echelons of the BND. You are familiar with this group, I assume?"

"Yes, sir," Brognola said, smiling with amusement. "I couldn't give you the German translation of the acronym to save my life, but I'm quite familiar with their operations. Former cold war espionage unit, now primary internal intelligence agency of the German Federal Republic. What's their angle in this?"

"Apparently, they know about your man's penetration of their country, and they're not happy about it. They've issued an order to shoot on sight."

"What?" Brognola bellowed.

A harsh glance from the President quieted him.

"For the moment, I have asked for some room on this, and explained his presence is at my personal request," the President continued. "That seems to have calmed them for the moment, but it pushes up the timetable considerably. We no longer have the luxury of waiting on this. I'm afraid we need to step up this operation. That's one of the reasons I decided to give you the specifications on the fighter. Basically, we don't have much time left."

"How much time?" Brognola asked, bracing himself for the answer.

"Seventy-two hours, give or take." The President sighed. "I'm sorry to dump this on you, Hal, but it's out of our hands. Once that time is up, I'm afraid your man is on his own. Let me be perfectly clear that after the seventy-two hour period, we no longer have sanctions, and you aren't authorized to attempt a rescue or extraction mission of any kind. Otherwise, the political ramifications could be devastating. Understood?"

"I understand, sir."

It wouldn't be the first time Bolan operated without sanction, but a shoot-on-sight order wasn't to be taken lightly.

The stakes had been raised. Brognola was going to have to act quickly if he was to save his friend. The President promised him the information would be sent via secured modem within the hour.

Brognola's drive back to Stony Man farm seemed to take an eternity.

THE WAR ROOM at Stony Man Farm was ominously silent.

Brognola's announcement rang in his ears like a death sentence, and the big Fed sat impatiently, wishing somebody would say something. He was prepared for the worst, and it was Aaron Kurtzman who finally broke the silence.

"Seventy-two hours?"

"And ten of them are already gone," Brognola retorted.

Kurtzman slammed his fist into his open palm. "That's not fair, Hal!"

"I know it's not fair, but it's out of the President's hands. This is a compromise he reached with the BND. It's politics, and the German authorities don't really care what's at stake."

"I don't believe it," Kurtzman protested. "I think the President sees Striker as a necessary evil at times. But I think they did this on purpose, and—"

"Now hold on, Bear," Brognola cautioned, raising his hand, "let's not start making accusations or jumping to conclusions."

"I agree with Hal," Barbara Price announced. "Regardless of the President's feelings for Striker, I don't think he would resort to treachery. I think we should concentrate on what we can do on this end to help our guy. What he needs most right now is our support. Especially with the lines of communication down."

"Agreed," Brognola replied.

"Sorry," Kurtzman added. "I guess I lost my head a little."

Price leaned over and placed her hand on his arm. "Don't worry about it. Let's just concentrate on what we know so far."

"Bear, did the information come through on the fighter?" Brognola asked.

"Yes, I have it all lined up for you," Kurtzman said as he turned toward a portable laptop. "A good portion of it is technical. I don't even understand a lot of it. I figured the best way to illustrate the true scope of this thing is to compare it to some of the most modern combat jet fighters currently in existence."

"Go ahead," Brognola interjected. "We're all ears."

"I'll put it on the viewer."

They spun in their chairs and concentrated on the wall screen at the front. Kurtzman plugged the downloaded information into his laptop computer, which then fed the information into the projector. Since his injuries had confined the computer expert to a wheelchair long ago, the high-tech equipment he had become accustomed to using, and designing, was state-of-the-art. He was one of the most intelligent and knowledgeable computer programmers in the world, as well as a crack information hacker.

The computer graphics imager spit a sleek silver aircraft on the screen. It had four wings—the two main wings, and two smaller ones at the tail—which were at right angles to the upright tail fins. The jet was stamped with U.S. Air Force markings.

"This is the F-14A Tomcat," Kurtzman said. "It's extremely fast, exceeding fifteen hundred miles per hour at an altitude of about forty thousand feet. It can engage up to six targets simultaneously, is armed with a 20 mm cannon, six Phoenix or Sparrow missiles, up to four Sidewinders, and can even carry bombs. Its engagement range is anywhere between one hundred and five hundred miles."

"Impressive," Price commented.

"It has to be," Brognola added, "considering it is currently the primary defense aircraft of the U.S."

"The other neat thing about it is when you compare it to the F/A-18 Hornet, which can only engage two fighters simultaneously. That's a three-to-one ratio."

Kurtzman tabbed the button on his laptop, and the image changed to a fighter painted flat black, with sleek lines, and an all-too-familiar shape. "The F-117 Nighthawk."

"The Stealth bomber," Barbara said, moderate surprise in her voice.

"Yes," Kurtzman continued. "Manufactured by Lockheed through a special project office contracted by the Department of Defense. It took almost seven years to design and build it, but its true speed has never really been disclosed, nor has its flight ceiling. It's estimated to exceed Mach 1. It can carry two AIM-9L air-to-air missiles, one-third the complement of the Tomcat, but its principal design was for bombing, and it has a load capacity for bombs that exceeds two tons."

Brognola whistled. "One of the most mysterious craft in the U.S. arsenal. Even our information is sketchy on it, and we have top secret access."

"It goes beyond the Pentagon," Kurtzman replied. He hit another key. "This is the F-16 Falcon. Another one of Lockheed's genius aircraft. It was originally designed by General Dynamics before Lockheed bought them out in 1993. Probably the most well-known, it's seen service domestically and abroad, including with NATO and in South and Central America. Its speed exceeds thirteen hundred miles per hour, and its weaponry includes Vulcan cannons and over ten tons in missiles that can engage ground and air targets. It's also extremely agile in combat, and was an invaluable resource during Desert Storm."

"I remember seeing some of the statistics of this aircraft before," Price interjected. "It flew something like thirteen thousand combined combat missions during the Gulf War, correct?''

''Yeah, it sure did,'' Kurtzman said. ''The Israelis love this ship. During the war in Lebanon, they shot down over forty Syrian MiGs, and they didn't lose a single aircraft on their side.''

''They were used quite effectively by the Israelis during the Gulf War, as well,'' Brognola commented.

''Aaron, how does this compare to Krizova's fighter?'' Price asked.

''Oh, now that is another whole story in itself,'' Kurtzman replied, flashing a wicked grin. ''But there's just one other plane you might want to know about before I give you the information on Krizova's fighter. It has a direct bearing on this new ship.''

''Okay,'' Brognola conceded, ''let have it.''

A tan-colored fighter filled the screen. ''This is the Jaguar GR.Mk 1A, currently in use by the French, and England's RAF. It's had a few radar and weapons upgrades since it first entered service in 1973, but it's no less impressive than the newer ships. The Jaguar is a twin-engine craft capable of speeds exceeding Mach 1.5. Although it has a limited range, its weaponry is impressive. It comes with twin 30 mm Aden cannons, two Sidewinders and a five-ton bomb-storage capacity on its underwings.''

Without warning, a new CGI enhancement came into view on the screen. It was a rough sketch, modeled in a blueprint form, with small technical data in balloons surrounding the aircraft sketch itself. Brognola and Price immediately knew they were staring at the new fighter. The room was filled with a sense of awe, and Kurtzman paused his narrative for effect, letting them take in the impressive sight.

''This is the new fighter, currently dubbed the K-1 Intercept Stealth Sortie. Actually, they're calling it KISS, for short. It uses a reflective matte-black exterior, modified from the Stealth, and is completely impervious to radar scans. Its weaponry will include quadruple 30 mm cannons, six AIM-9L Sidewinders and a seven-ton reserve-bomb capacity. Fully loaded, its estimated speed will be somewhere in the area of Mach 3.5 to 4.''

"My God," Brognola whispered. "That's over twenty-five hundred miles per hour."

"Twenty-six hundred sixty at sea level and room temperature, to be precise," Kurtzman declared. "This fighter could fly from here to Europe in just under three hours, and it's nearly capable of outrunning a CRV-7 rocket. It will also have a precision guidance system, personally developed by Krizova, which promises to surpass anything in existence. The only downside is it must slow down in order to achieve lock, and it requires a crew of three. The other thing is the expense of production. At those atmospheric speeds, the hull has to be made of a certain alloy, a complicated formula that only Krizova knows."

"I would assume that's what he used as his bargaining chip?" Price asked.

"Probably," Brognola replied with a nod. "I'm not exactly up on all this modern technology, but it's no secret we've been capable of attaining those speeds for years. The problem is not how we go that fast."

Kurtzman nodded, finishing the statement. "It's how we keep from blowing apart at the seams when we do. Krizova seems to have found that answer."

"This might seem a bit off track right now," Price stated, "but how do we know this isn't some kind of scam?"

"I'd ask the same question, Barb," Brognola replied, "except I personally believe this is very real. Obviously, the President believes it, because we have already seen his desperation in matters of security. It was our assessment that if this weapon, or even the knowledge of such a weapon, fell into the wrong hands, the whole world could be at risk.''

''Well, now that we know what kind of technology we're talking about, how does that pinpoint possible considerations in Krizova's abduction?'' Kurtzman asked.

''I began looking into that when we first received this information,'' Price announced, producing a thick manila envelope from her briefcase. ''All intelligence reports inside Europe indicate it's a terrorist group that could have been behind the abduction and murders of our Japanese liaisons.''

''Terrorists?'' Brognola reiterated, his eyebrows arching. ''In Germany?''

Price nodded. ''The BND and Czech police are convinced this man is behind the work in Prague.'' She pulled a glossy black-and-white photograph from the folder and slid it across the table.

Brognola snatched it up and studied the photograph carefully. The man was big and tall, with light hair, and dressed in military fatigues. He stood next to another man, and they appeared to be talking conspiratorially.

''The taller man,'' Price went on, ''is Dortmund Linger, a well-known mercenary in the underworld today. He is a former BND operative, and said to be a quick and methodical killer. Very professional and very dangerous. The man next to him is his second-in-command, Niktor Hess.''

''What else do we know about him?''

''Not much, I'm afraid,'' Price replied, ''although recent reports state he's resurfaced in Germany.''

''That sounds a bit too close for coincidence,'' Kurtzman pondered aloud.

''Affirmative on that,'' Brognola stated. He tossed the photograph on the table and added, ''It's a place to start, anyway. I imagine the information you've compiled on Linger is in that folder?''

''Yes.''

''It seems the only question now is how we get it inside Frankfurt, find Striker and give it to him.''

''I've been considering our options,'' Brognola replied. ''At first, I was inclined to pull out all the stops and send in Phoenix Force. They're on another mission, though, and I can't justify pulling them out.''

''Plus, it's not like we can just fax this stuff over to our friends at the CIA office in Frankfurt,'' Kurtzman added.

''That's for sure,'' Price agreed. ''The American intelligence community today has eyes and ears everywhere, and they seem to be finding it increasingly difficult to keep their mouths shut. We have to get this to Striker personally.''

Brognola was silent for a short time, thinking furiously. Considering the situation, and their timetable, he thought he had a solution. There was one man who had worked with Bolan many times. He also had knowledge and talents uniquely suited to this particular mission, and he would go the distance to find and help the Executioner.

''Bear,'' Brognola finally said, ''get me Jack Grimaldi.''

6

Frankfurt

Dr. Vasec Krizova couldn't concentrate. Thoughts of Mila filled his head constantly, and he was tormented with dreams of what she had to be suffering at the hands of her captors. Worse yet, Krizova wasn't completely sure of where his daughter was being held. But one thing was certain—he wouldn't be able to stall forever.

In less than a month, Krizova had constructed an aircraft that should have taken months to build. Linger's crews worked constantly to build the winged bird of death, and construction of the cockpit was all that remained. Fortunately, some of the materials Linger had purchased through the black market wouldn't be sufficient. That would create a realistic delay. He didn't relish telling the big blond German about the faulty electronics. It would only make the man angrier, and Krizova didn't have time to deal with that anger.

Vasec Krizova had dealt with enough hatred and violence in his life. His government was neither forgiving nor patient. Bureaucrats were impetuous people, given to rash decisions with no forethought of the consequences. Krizova had spent the prime years of his life as a scientist, and his aspirations had been twisted to suit the purposes of the men he had worked for.

In the years following his formal education, Krizova had

learned that man was basically evil. He wished for the simpler life he'd once known, working for a private company in a laboratory. He wished his beloved Marta were still alive. His late wife had been his reason for living; she had been his purpose to strive for excellence. Now, Mila was that purpose. Krizova would have built a million fighters for his daughter, but he had to be realistic. There was no earthly way Schleyer and Linger could let him live once the fighter was completed.

Krizova didn't care anymore. He couldn't remember a time he actually did care. His life was over, and the best he could hope for was the safety of his daughter. Linger was nothing but a cold-blooded killer, but Edel Schleyer seemed to be a man of some integrity. At least, it made him feel better to tell himself that.

The Czech scientist couldn't help feel saddened by the loss of the Japanese businessmen who had offered to buy the design plans. They had died senselessly. They were no threat to Schleyer, yet Linger had killed them without blinking an eye. He had commanded that their throats be slit, forcing Vasec and Mila to watch. From that moment, Krizova regretted his decision to reveal his invention. He had repeatedly seen his own government turn his creative genius toward the destruction of other human beings. They had twisted his work to serve their own subversive aims.

Krizova could only make an educated guess about who the real buyers were. The Japanese couldn't create weapons, and the jet was a true weapon of war. They either wanted the plans to resell, or they had been trying to protect their own interests. Without the firepower and advanced guidance system, his jet could be used to further the cause of peace. In the right hands, it might still meet that end. However, in the hands of the Iron Skull, Krizova's creation would only become another destructive tool of terrorism.

The scientist looked up from the table as the head of one

of the technical crews approached. The man's name was Heiner, a burly man with curly black hair and dark eyes. Krizova had to supervise a dozen crew chiefs, as well as a handful of actual technicians. He couldn't help but be impressed with Schleyer's resources. The technicians working under the Czech had degrees from some of the most prominent schools in Europe, and even a few from the United States.

Although Heiner was just another Iron Skull stooge, he was pleasant enough. He had never attempted to use his size or experience to intimidate Krizova as Linger had done.

"Dr. Krizova?" Heiner greeted him respectfully.

"Yes, Heiner, what is it?"

"We are having trouble with the guidance system hook-ups. It looks like possibly another faulty converter."

"Another one?" Krizova let out a deep sigh. "That's the fourth one. Is *all* of the equipment your commander purchased faulty?"

"I have no idea," Heiner said, "but this module burned out, as well."

Krizova paused to give the problem serious thought, turning to the electrical schematics on the table. He knew the fighter inside out. He didn't really have to refer to his design plans, but it helped him to push the thoughts of Mila from his conscience. He looked back at Heiner.

"It has to be in the wiring. I cannot believe all the power-converter modules are bad. Expose channels four and five, and I will be over in a minute to look it over."

"Yes, Doctor," Heiner replied dutifully.

"Dr. Krizova," a cultured voice called behind him.

Krizova whirled to see Edel Schleyer standing there. Linger towered above the German businessman, flanking him like a granite statue. Krizova actually experienced some relief. He preferred to deal with Schleyer rather than Linger's sinister presence.

Schleyer stepped up to the table and looked over the plans casually.

As if he knew what he was looking at, Krizova thought.

"I trust all is going well?" Schleyer remarked.

"I would not necessarily say that, Herr Schleyer," Krizova replied, casting a haughty glance in Linger's direction.

The mercenary scowled at Krizova, and the scientist redirected his attention to Schleyer.

"Oh?" Schleyer prompted.

"Thus far, three of the converter modules Commander Linger supplied have burned up in the preliminary power tests. I am not yet certain if it is an overload in the wiring system or if the modules are faulty. My initial conclusions lead me to think the latter."

"Commander, what is the meaning of this?" Schleyer asked, turning an accusatory look toward Linger.

"There is nothing wrong with the modules," Linger said. "My sources are reliable. I think the doctor is stalling."

"Well," Schleyer concluded, throwing up his arms, "there you have it. Commander Linger says you are stalling, Dr. Krizova. Is that true?"

Krizova's expression was one of hatred. Schleyer was playing two ends against the middle. The man was indeed crafty. He knew how much Krizova despised Linger. The scientist feared for his daughter's life—a life Linger had threatened repeatedly. Schleyer was aware of this, and he was using it to his advantage.

Krizova decided to take another approach.

"Herr Schleyer, I will of course look at all of my options. If I have learned anything as a scientist, it is to never make assumptions. Nevertheless, I have tested this system before and never had this problem. I cannot be expected to supervise every single facet of the fighter's production, and I am convinced my calculations are correct.''

"Yes, Doctor, you *can* be expected to supervise every part of the construction, and you will,'' Schleyer said quietly. He walked up to Krizova and patted the scientist's shoulder. "I have full confidence you will perform to my satisfaction.''

Schleyer became silent. He didn't have to say anything more. The threat was obvious in the man's tone of voice. Krizova heard the words, but he could also interpret the meaning. He would perform to Schleyer's satisfaction, or else....

"That does not completely solve our problem,'' Krizova protested. "If the module converters *are* bad, I will need more of them. Until I can determine the cause, we must expect more burnouts. I cannot test the equipment without them, and the fighter's guidance system will not work properly without them. If you wish me to complete the project, then give me the proper equipment.''

"I will get you more of these things, Doctor,'' Schleyer replied, his smile gone now. "I will get you a thousand. I will get you ten thousand, if that's what it takes, but you will complete this project on time.''

"I will do my best.''

"You had better do more than that,'' Schleyer muttered. "Your time is almost up.''

THE EXECUTIONER WATCHED from the Dodge Aries as Dan Lincoln entered the main train station at Frankfurt. As promised, he had called four hours after the original meet and instructed Lincoln to meet him. A public place seemed an odd choice for this kind of rendezvous, but Bolan couldn't take any chances.

If Jütta Kaufmann had been correct, Bolan couldn't trust anybody at the CIA. Lincoln seemed agreeable enough, but common sense dictated he take such precautions. The soldier hadn't been keen on the idea of using the Company as a liaison in such a sensitive mission to begin with, but Brognola had made it clear the decision was out of their hands. Bolan might have refused the mission, but he knew what was at stake. His job was to assess the risks and take action, and that suited the Executioner well enough. It would have served no purpose to argue the point.

After waiting to insure Lincoln hadn't been tailed, Bolan left the car and strolled across the street. He had changed into tan slacks, a white shirt and a sleeveless red sweater. A tan suit coat concealed the Beretta 93-R, tucked in shoulder leather with the selector switch set for 3-round bursts. A small briefcase he carried contained the .44 Magnum Desert Eagle.

The main station was crowded, the noontime rush evident as Bolan maneuvered through the throngs. The sounds of hurried travel echoed, almost drowning out the indecipherable announcements spewing from ancient loudspeakers. A very high, cathedral-like ceiling blended those sounds far above the activity.

Bolan found Lincoln sitting at the rendezvous spot, a portable bistro facing the tracks. He sat next to Lincoln, who was nursing a beer, and ordered a coffee. When the bar attendant had delivered the drink and moved out of earshot, Bolan spoke in a low voice.

"Did you reach my people?"

"Yes, I did," Lincoln replied, keeping his eyes forward. "They confirmed everything you said, and I was to provide you with whatever you need. They also said to tell you to proceed as planned."

"Fine. Did you bring the equipment I requested?"

Lincoln shook his head. "That wasn't as easy, but I've taken care of it. We have a contact who will deliver it later tonight, and will also have more information."

Bolan's eyes flashed with suspicion. "That wasn't the deal."

"What can I tell you, Belasko?" Lincoln said, looking at Bolan and shrugging. "That's the best I could do on short notice. You want the stuff, you have to wait for it. Like I told your people, we're kind of short-handed right now. I have two dead agents to deal with. What more do you want?"

"What do you mean 'two dead agents'?" Bolan snapped, changing the subject. "I'm only aware of one."

"I received a call shortly after you left. The Czech police found Carter's body in a forest outside Prague. Those bastards shot him in the head. They stripped him nude and executed him."

Bolan fell silent. There was no longer a question in his mind. Someone had been privy to the meeting in Prague and kidnapped the Krizovas. Wiley had probably been followed from Frankfurt, or even forced into disclosing the details of the meet. The work had been quick and methodical, just the kind of military efficiency that confirmed Kaufmann's conclusions about Linger's involvement. Someone else had to be pulling the strings, though, someone with the far-reaching connections and resources to initiate such a strategy.

The name Schleyer came to Bolan's mind.

"I'm sorry to hear about Wiley. My sources told me he was a good man."

"He was," Lincoln replied. His attitude toward Bolan was hardly friendly.

"What about this contact of yours?" Bolan asked.

Lincoln pulled a piece of paper from his coat and slid it to Bolan. "Her name is Gabi. She'll meet you at the Sachsenhausen district at 2100 hundred hours. It's in the southern part of Frankfurt, over the Main River. Can you find it?"

"Yeah," Bolan replied, pocketing the paper without glancing at it. "I'll manage. Watch yourself, Lincoln."

"Sure. I'll be heading for Prague immediately, so I won't be in touch for a while. If you need anything else, Gabi should be able to take care of it."

"That's fine with me. Good luck."

Bolan walked away from the bistro and headed back to his car. Within minutes, he was in the Aries and cruising toward Griesheim. He needed to talk with Jütta Kaufmann to get more information on Dortmund Linger. The BND agent turned mercenary was the only definitive link, and his best chance of finding Krizova. Even if his suspicions about this Schleyer were true, Linger was still the starting point.

The information in the file folder provided by Dan Lincoln had been sketchy. Even as Bolan had studied it, he realized the mistakes his government had made. The first forty-eight hours had been crucial, and it still took more than three weeks before the President acted. Bolan didn't care to try to second-guess decisions that were already made. He knew there was nothing he could do about it. He had enough to go on, and the objective was clear now. The axioms of war were the only kind of thing men like Linger understood, and Bolan was more than ready to deliver.

As he rounded the corner of Kaufmann's street, his combat senses came alive.

A quick jerk of the steering wheel was the only thing that saved him, as the street in front of him erupted with a fiery flash. A large chunk of concrete broke the windshield, obscuring Bolan's view. The Aries careened onto the sidewalk and struck a telephone pole. He gritted his teeth as his knees slammed into the dash, the pain shooting up his legs inside the compact vehicle.

The soldier shook off the agony, pulling the Desert Eagle from the briefcase on the passenger floor as flames rose up from the edges of the mangled hood. He quickly exited the vehicle, willing himself to stand on his numbed legs. Through the smoke and heat of the twisted wreckage, Bolan could barely make out a figure crouched across the street. The man was popping a grenade into an M-79 launcher.

The Executioner angled away from the car, sighting his .44 Magnum on the grenadier. He squeezed the trigger twice, the big gun booming as it rocked in Bolan's steady grip. The .44 rounds connected, blowing out large sections of the grenadier's chest. The body back-flipped, striking the grassy curb in front of Jütta Kaufmann's apartment building with tremendous impact.

Bolan scanned the courtyard beyond the waist-high fence encircling the building, already tracking his pistol on a second target. The gunman burst from hiding behind a storage shed at the near side of the courtyard, raising his Uzi machine pistol. A wind gust blew smoke into Bolan's eyes a second before he stroked the trigger. The slug went high, and Bolan cursed as he sprawled on the pavement. The gunner's shots burned empty air above him.

The soldier rolled twice and came up in a crouch as more of the Uzi rounds ricocheted off the pavement nearby. The Desert Eagle thundered as Bolan nailed his target, the 230-grain round drilling through the man's upper lip and blowing the back of his head apart. The corpse stood erect a few seconds before toppling to the ground.

Bolan swept the pistol left and right, bracing himself for further resistance. As the echoes of the gunfire died, the sound of crackling flames reached his ears. The car's interior was totally engulfed. He crossed the gap to the trunk to try to retrieve the weapons he'd transferred from the Citroën, but the smoke and heat were too intense, and the keys were still inside.

Before the soldier could decide on an alternate plan, the windows on the fourth floor of the apartment building blew out, sending flaming stone and deadly shards of glass in all directions. Bolan's eyes widened in surprise. His attackers hadn't been after him. He had simply stumbled onto their real purpose. They had come to kill Kaufmann!

Screeching tires assaulted his senses, and Bolan turned, dropping to one knee and sighting his Desert Eagle on the next threat. The sporty car was a dark blue two-door hatchback, and Bolan could make out the beautiful, familiar face through the dirty windshield. The car ground to a halt and nearly fell into the hole left by the M-79's high-explosive shell.

Jütta Kaufmann rolled down her window, a cigarette dangling between her lips. "Hey there, soldier!"

Bolan lowered his pistol, immediately rising and running to her. "Move over!" he ordered.

A brief glance at the devastation was enough to convince Kaufmann it was neither the time nor place to argue with him.

As she climbed over the stick shift and Bolan slid behind the wheel, the Aries's windows blew out. Bolan didn't wait to adjust the seat, careful not to bang his bruised knees on the dash as he threw the gear lever into reverse and popped the clutch. Bolan picked up speed, powering the hatchback car into a perfect J-turn at the intersection. As the sounds of secondary explosions faded, Bolan checked the rearview mirror.

There were no signs of pursuit.

He turned to look at the BND agent staring hard at her with a mixture of surprise and relief. She smiled at him, and Bolan returned a brief grin of his own before becoming serious.

"I thought you were dead," Bolan said.

"So did I," Kaufmann replied. "Fortunately, I saw those guys watching the place earlier. That was after I woke up and found you gone.

"I wasn't sure what they were up to," she continued, "but I left the apartment to see if they would follow me."

"Apparently, rigging a bomb in your apartment was more important," Bolan concluded. "It looks like your search for Linger is over."

"What do you mean?"

"Carter Wiley's body was found outside of Prague today. My people know what's going on, and I'm convinced Linger is a main player. The opposition's movements are too precise for me to think otherwise. They're using military weapons which I think are being supplied by someone named Schleyer."

Kaufmann looked surprised. "Schleyer? Edel Schleyer?"

"I don't know for sure, but one of the hired guns I encountered at Wiley's apartment early this morning dropped that name."

"Yes, I figured that was your handiwork," Kaufmann remarked with a disarming grin. "If it *is* Edel Schleyer, you have your work cut out for you."

7

The Sachsenhausen underworld was a part of Frankfurt that most Germans would have preferred not to admit existing. Although culturally different from the bowels of New York City, the principal idea was the same. In no other part of the city was business greater for the Turkish selling hash, the women selling sex and the bistro owners selling whatever was left. That included some of the finest and purest alcoholic brews in the world.

American GIs formerly stationed there would joke, saying, "Sachsenhausen is blocks of bars, floors of whores." It had once been the main hangout for American servicemen, and the chief cause of problems for the police and MPs alike. Nevertheless, it was there and the vices of its inhabitants readily available.

Since the fall of the Berlin Wall, things had changed tremendously in Germany. Jobs were scarce, as opening the border between East and West sent scores of East Germans rushing into the arms of their more productive counterpart. It was amazing what hunger, unemployment and poverty could do to motivate the human race to reach for higher goals. Others took to selling whatever was most popular at the moment, not caring who was on the receiving end or what long-term effects such sales might have.

It was the kind of prostitution Mack Bolan understood.

The Executioner understood it, but he didn't always agree with it. Three women had already propositioned him in the fifty minutes since his arrival. He politely declined each of them. He wasn't their judge, and he didn't really care. His meeting with the mysterious woman he knew only as Gabi was the highlight of the evening—she was already late.

He sat in a corner booth, dark enough to go relatively unnoticed but providing himself with a perfect view of the rest of the bar. A lukewarm beer sat in front of him, a lemon floating on top. Bolan had barely touched it. In his life, where the tendency for sudden violence required him to be always alert and ready, there was no room for alcohol to dim his senses.

As Bolan watched the door for any sign of his contact, he turned his thoughts to Jütta Kaufmann. After a quick trip to the BND office to acquire all known intelligence reports on Edel Schleyer, they had returned to Bolan's motel and studied the information on Schleyer. The man was quite successful in both his domestic and international business dealings. He was respected by the German government and held tight political ties within the country.

His financial empire apparently spread far and wide. He owned five homes, all in different countries, and his company was the parent to seventeen separate firms that did business on six continents. The one conclusion that Bolan could draw was Schleyer didn't like America. He didn't have a residence on American soil, or in an American-controlled territory, and he didn't do business with Americans.

One local paper noted that Schleyer had personally turned down a multimillion-dollar sales option to the influential American billionaire tycoon, Robert James Yates. The stunning part was that it would have made Schleyer billions of dollars and been one of the most shrewd and cunning business moves in history. In other words, a no-lose situation for Schleyer. Yet the German businessman had adamantly refused, citing some obscure reason for his decision, and the subject was closed. In the business world, Schleyer's choice had been considered nothing less than economical suicide.

Otherwise, the guy was clean.

Bolan wasn't buying it. He was convinced Schleyer was involved in Krizova's disappearance, and considered the possibility that Schleyer's proposal had been the anonymous one Krizova reportedly had turned down. It would make sense. A proud German like Schleyer wouldn't be able to handle such a blow to his ego. If Schleyer had been behind Krizova's kidnapping, it would stand to reason that he was keeping Krizova alive for a more sinister purpose. It would also confirm Bolan's suspicions that someone was financing Linger's personal army, and pulling the strings in the American intelligence community.

It was all falling into place.

A strikingly beautiful woman entered the bar, and Bolan's heartbeat increased. The flared hips, the silky hair of fiery reds and browns, the full figure and confident gait— the woman bore an uncanny resemblance to his lost love, April Rose.

The woman's luminous eyes ran across the bar, stopping when they met Bolan's penetrating stare. She immediately strolled over and sat across from him at the greasy wooden table. Her eyes seemed to glow, even in the dim light of the bar. German rock music blared from the distant jukebox, but it was far enough away that they could talk quietly.

After studying Bolan for a moment, the woman spoke, her throaty voice clipped but quite sultry. "You are just as Herr Lincoln described you."

"That's funny. He didn't describe you at all."

"He has other matters on his mind," she replied.

"Yeah. Do you have the equipment I requested?"

She nodded. "It's not here, but I will take you to it."

"Do you want a beer?"

"Ja, danke schön."

Bolan slid out of the booth and walked to the bar. Within a minute, he returned with a glass and a bottle of beer. Gabi Reinmaul poured the beer, canting the glass at an angle to achieve the perfect one-inch head of foam the Germans seemed so fixated on.

Bolan got down to business. "What information do you have for me?"

"Herr Lincoln tells me you mentioned the name Schleyer. It did not mean anything to him."

"But it means a lot to you?" Bolan concluded.

"Jawohl. If it is the same man. His full name is Edel Schleyer, and he is a prominent man in this country. And a powerful one."

"I have my own doubts about him," Bolan replied.

"You mean to say suspicions, yes?" Reinmaul asked.

Bolan nodded.

"I know Edel Schleyer. Personally." There was a trace of anger in the woman's voice, and she leaned closer to Bolan. "I believe your assumptions are correct. I think I can help you."

"I'm listening."

Reinmaul leaned back in her seat and studied Bolan quietly before continuing. "Edel Schleyer and I were involved once. He is well connected in the political world, and quite influential in many circles throughout Europe. Money is the key to his power, and he has much of it. He is virtually unreachable. He is married, actually, and I was his mistress. I cut it off when he wanted to put me away. I told him I was carrying his child."

"I'm not concerned with the extent of your relationship. I need something I can use against this clown."

"Oh, I assure you, Herr Belasko," Reinmaul countered, "Edel Schleyer is no clown. He would order your life snuffed out in a moment if he knew you were here looking for him.''

''Apparently, he already does,'' Bolan said.

Reinmaul nodded. ''I have heard the reports of your activities. There is another man named Linger. A mercenary who serves as Edel's enforcer. This man is very devoted to Edel, and he would kill for him, I think.''

''He's already killed for him,'' Bolan shot back. ''Many times. Including a CIA agent named Carter Wiley. I intend to make sure both Schleyer and Linger account for that.''

''You will need your own army, then,'' the woman replied.

''I think I can handle it.''

There was a long silence, as Gabrielle Reinmaul appeared to ponder Bolan's words. The Executioner could tell she was holding back, but he didn't want to press her too hard. It wasn't for his sake that she hesitated, but probably for her own. Bolan surmised it was only natural. She was obviously afraid for her own life. If Schleyer somehow managed to stop Bolan, he would surely find out that Reinmaul had been the one talking. Bolan figured his best tack would be to back off. The woman's conscience would dictate her involvement.

''I have no allegiance to Edel Schleyer,'' she finally said. ''I can tell you how to find him, but that is where I must stop. He would kill me if he found out.''

''I'll do what I can to protect you.''

Reinmaul laughed. ''Do not make rash promises you could not keep, Herr Belasko.'' She looked around, then lowered her voice. ''We should not talk here anymore. We have been here too long. Come, and I will take you to the guns.''

After leaving the bar, she led Bolan down an alleyway to her waiting vehicle. It was a black BMW, with leather interior and all the options. Bolan looked at Reinmaul with some surprise mixed with suspicion. His expression wasn't lost on her.

"A gift," she explained. "From Edel."

Reinmaul drove them out of Sachsenhausen and across the bridge to the northern city. Bolan's eyes flicked to the side mirrors, looking for tails. It was getting late, and the traffic had thinned considerably. He still felt something in his gut that he could not explain.

The whole meet had smelled of a setup. He stole glances at Reinmaul's profile in the dark, illuminated only by the blue-white of the dash lights. Bolan couldn't shake the uncanny resemblance. Something didn't feel right. There was nothing furtive or nervous about the woman's manner, no sense of betrayal in her voice. Nevertheless, Bolan was listening to his instincts. He would have to be on his guard.

They crossed the bridge, and Reinmaul made a right. The road began to narrow, dropping steadily toward the level of the river, which was now barely visible through Bolan's side window. The reflection of bridge and house lights shimmered on the dark and peaceful waters.

Bolan's hand slid under his jacket to the cold butt of the Beretta, his eyes never leaving the road as he spoke. "Where are we going?"

"Herr Lincoln said that you needed weapons," she replied, smiling. "I am taking you to them. You are a very nervous man, *ja?*"

"I prefer to call it cautious," Bolan replied tightly.

They soon reached the river bottom. Reinmaul made another hard right, leaving the road and driving along a bumpy dirt road of gravel, sand and packed mud. The deciduous trees enclosing the path were thick and full, fed by the unceasing waters of the river. The tips of some of their branches whipped at the sides of the BMW or snapped against the corners of the windshield. The road suddenly opened into a small clearing, and Reinmaul shut off the lights.

She reached into the back seat, and Bolan tensed, but she only produced two flashlights with red lenses. She handed one to him, then silently gestured for him to follow her. They got out of the car, and he followed her about fifty yards through the clearing and down another path. Their journey finally ended at a wooden shed measuring two hundred square feet. The shed had a small, padlocked door.

"Kind of a strange place to keep guns, isn't it?" Bolan asked.

Reinmaul touched his hand holding the flashlight and Bolan felt his hand tingle with the touch. She guided him to point the flashlight close to the padlock, put her finger to her lips, then dug in her pocket to withdraw the padlock key. She opened the shed, then flicked on her flashlight and stepped inside. Bolan followed in behind her, closing the door behind them. A moment later, the shed was bathed in the soft glow of a kerosene lantern, and Bolan saw his weapons.

The muzzles of four Steyr MPi69 submachine guns stared back at Bolan.

Gabrielle Reinmaul stood behind the gunmen, her arms folded and smiling with satisfaction as Bolan met her gaze. He had fallen into a trap, even after warning himself against such an event. Bolan cursed himself for allowing the woman to dupe him, and he considered his options—he had none. The four gunmen had the drop on him, and they stood at a distance that made close-quarters combat out of the question. Unless he could find a distraction.

Mack Bolan tightened his grip on the flashlight.

AGENT JÜTTA KAUFMANN LIT another cigarette as she checked her watch.

It would still be some time before Belasko returned, and

she was scheduled for a meeting with the commissioner in one hour. Kaufmann knew what her superior wanted more than anything else. He wanted her, and he had never made any secret about it with his weak passes and reptilian manners. Kaufmann tried not to let the idea bother her. She was quite aware that such things happened daily to German women in the business world. The old German culture didn't look well upon women in the intelligence and law-enforcement community.

In the Federal Republic of Germany, intelligence, security and policing were the jobs of men, and a woman in the field was rare. Although the country's laws didn't allow for discrimination against women in the field, such prejudices occurred on a daily basis all over the country, especially in the bigger cities. Kaufmann had worked long and hard to rise to her status in the BND. She wasn't about to let her boss ruin that, so she tolerated his advances if it put her closer to rising through the ranks. Eventually, she would rise to the rank of commander, and transfer out of Frankfurt.

Perhaps Stuttgart would be better. Or even Berlin.

Kaufmann drove thoughts of work troubles from her head and tried to concentrate on the material regarding Edel Schleyer. Although Belasko didn't have any hard evidence, the agent thought the big soldier was onto something.

Edel Schleyer's businesses were all legitimate, and his holdings were vast. He had never been known to fraternize with those who weren't deemed honest businessmen in both the domestic and international circles. Schleyer was renowned for his generosity with money, donating to several worthy charities on a regular basis, and throwing a monthly gala at his large estate in Frankfurt. He had never been charged with any crime, let alone arrested, and he was in good standing with nearly every bank in Europe and Asia.

Kaufmann was about to give up when she found an

American magazine clipping that had been attached to the copy of a bill of sale. It was an article on Schleyer's inheritance of a castle that was south of the city. The article talked about Schleyer's love for the castle, originally purchased by his grandfather in 1900. The tourist magazine had apparently done an exposé on the castle, comparing it to others throughout Germany and the Scottish Highlands. Something clicked in the woman's head, and she went back to a carbon copy of a bill of sale that had been filed for many acres of land surrounding the castle.

It was quite a bit of land, a rare commodity in Germany, the purchase of which was reserved only for the very wealthy or those who could do something prosperous with it. The purchase had apparently been made secondhand, the proceeds from each purchase moved through several banks. In fact, it was a tremendous amount of land. Enough land to house…an army? Perhaps.

She was beginning to see a pattern and decided to go visit the area later to see what she could find out. It was time for her meeting with the commissioner.

Kaufmann took the U-Bahn to the heart of the downtown area. The BND office was an eight-story building located on Friedberger Landstrasse, a major thoroughfare through the heart of the governmental district. Security was tight. Once she made it past the usual checks, she took the elevator to her office on the sixth floor, returning the files on Schleyer. When she had finished, she made her way to the top floor of the office complex, arriving three minutes early for her meeting.

The floor was deserted, most of the lights that normally illuminated the circular room of desks and cubicles were off, and only a dim glow came from the glass enclosure that marked the commissioner's office. She crossed the expanse, knocking briefly and entering only when she heard a grumbled assent from behind the door.

Commissioner Baldric Gerhard looked up from his desk. The usual jovial smile wasn't present. He sat behind his desk, jacket off and tossed carelessly on a chair in one corner, his shirtsleeves rolled halfway up his thick forearms. He was balding, with a shock of white hair and a smooth face. Beady little eyes peered out from the large, egg-shaped face.

Gerhard gestured to the seat in front of his desk, and Kaufmann took her seat quickly and quietly. Gerhard studied her resolutely for the longest time, and she fought back the urge to squirm in her seat. Normally, the old man would practically be all over her by now. Not this time. There was something in his expression that she didn't like, and Kaufmann wasn't sure she really wanted to know what was on his mind.

Maybe, just maybe, she would quickly be able to give her report and leave.

"Agent Kaufmann, I am very disappointed in you," Gerhard said. "You have truly betrayed me."

"I do not understand, Commissioner Gerhard," she replied, only a little surprised at his gruff tone.

"Do you understand *this?*" Gerhard said, snapping a photograph from his desk drawer and holding it out for her to see. It was a picture of her and the American entering her apartment.

Kaufmann looked up, her eyes widened. "You have had my apartment under surveillance?"

"Yes, indeed," Gerhard replied. "It is part of our ongoing investigation against Dortmund Linger's sympathizers within our organization."

"And you suspect me?" she asked with disbelief.

"Naturally. You have violated every trust we placed in you. You have deliberately disobeyed orders, and harbored a fugitive from your country." Gerhard tapped the figure of Bolan for emphasis. "This Mike Belasko is a dangerous man and considered an enemy of both Germany and everything it stands for. He has already been responsible for the deaths of several people, and spread a virtual panic through this city.''

''He was provoked,'' Kaufmann said bitterly. ''They attacked him first.''

''That is not the point, Agent Kaufmann!'' Gerhard shouted, jumping from his chair and slamming a meaty fist on his desk. ''He is a fugitive and a vigilante, and you have allied yourself with him by assisting him in his mission, whatever that might be.'' Gerhard lowered his voice and took his seat. ''I would like an explanation.''

''I was ordered to find Commander Linger and eliminate him,'' Kaufmann announced.

''Do not lecture me, Agent Kaufmann,'' Gerhard warned. ''I am well aware of what you were assigned to do.''

''Herr Belasko has promised to help me with that. I am only using him to get to Linger.''

''I wish I could believe that, but I do not,'' Gerhard said. ''After I ordered internal surveillance to commence, it was also brought to my attention that you pulled information concerning Edel Schleyer. I would assume that you have some evidence that implicates Herr Schleyer?''

Kaufmann didn't immediately reply. She had been betrayed by her own people—put under constant surveillance like a common criminal. It did confirm that she had definitely raised some eyebrows. She was becoming convinced that her theory about Schleyer hiding a private army in or near his castle was feasible, but she wasn't about to disclose this information to Gerhard. Nobody could be trusted. Linger had his claws on someone within the BND, and until she knew who it was, nobody was above suspicion, including her own superiors.

Kaufmann decided to keep her mouth shut.

"I believed there was a connection at first, but I now find the idea crazy and repulsive. I was caught believing a lie, a scrap bit of information I received, and I looked into it. As far as Mike Belasko is concerned, I can use him to get at Linger. However, I need time."

Gerhard sat back in his chair, pressing his fingertips together and studying her over them. Kaufmann could see the wheels turning. Gerhard was trying to find a way to put her off, but she knew he couldn't resist the chance to take credit for bringing down Dortmund Linger. It didn't matter who pulled the trigger. Linger had eluded the BND for years, and this was Gerhard's chance to further his career. There was no way he could pass it up.

"Very well," Gerhard finally replied. "There was a termination order on this Belasko, but it has been rescinded for another forty-eight hours. I have orders from the highest authority that he is not to be touched. This is a fortunate occurrence for you. I have no choice but to wait. Be aware, though, that he is fair game when that time is up. Will that satisfy you?"

"I promise to deliver, Commissioner," Kaufmann purred. "In more ways than one. You must trust me, though, and call off the surveillance. I can bring you two birds with one stone. I can bring you Dortmund Linger and Mike Belasko. You must believe me."

"I will wait. I will give you your chance to prove your innnocence."

"Thank you."

"Now, on another matter," Gerhard said, opening a file folder on his cluttered desk. "An operative from our counterintelligence office in Berlin states that a man was observed leaving Dulles Airport in Washington, D.C. The man is posing as a Lufthansa pilot, but reports indicate he is actually an operative being sent to assist Belasko. We do not have a description, but he is traveling under the name of Joseph Grimes, which I suspect is most likely an alias.''

"Why should this matter?" Kaufmann asked with a shrug.

"The man himself does not pose a threat," Gerhard grumbled. "It is the cargo he's carrying that we are concerned about. Our agents feel there are most likely weapons aboard that flight. I am sure the American government's intelligence operatives pulled some strings to get that equipment aboard. We have offered a reprieve for Belasko, but I'm sure you're aware we cannot tolerate the smuggling of munitions or other such contraband into our country. This violates our national security.''

"What do you want me to do?"

"I want you to intercept this man." Gerhard handed her an index card. "Here is the pertinent flight information, as well as a description of Herr Grimes and his cargo. You are to arrest him immediately upon his arrival, and confiscate any cargo or luggage he might be traveling with. Naturally, we will turn him over to the local CIA office for immediate return to the United States. He is *not* to be harmed in any way. I do not wish to start any incidents, if you understand.''

"I understand perfectly, Commissioner," Kaufmann replied. "I will not let you down.''

"I trust you won't," Gerhard huffed. "I am not entirely comfortable with your involvement in Belasko's operations here in Frankfurt. I will assume you have the situation under control, and that I need not interfere?''

"I promise not to become involved with Herr Belasko beyond a professional level, Commissioner Gerhard. Once I have Linger, I will take care of Belasko, just as you have ordered.''

"See that you do," Gerhard replied.

As the agent left the BND headquarters, she smiled at

the thought of breaking that promise. She could no more
bring herself to eliminate Mike Belasko than she could a
young child. It was unfortunate to think the elusive Belasko
would accidentally slip through her fingers unscathed.

The very thought of it was amusing.

8

The Executioner sprang into action seconds after the light came on.

A gunman stood in each opposing corner, with guns trained on him, and two directly in front, shielding Gabrielle Reinmaul. The gunmen didn't notice the kerosene lantern dangling directly above them.

Mack Bolan did.

The flashlight left his grip with startling speed, arcing across the space between himself and the lantern in less than a second. The lantern left the hook at the same moment as the soldier dodged to his right, in the direction of the youngest and most inexperienced-looking hardman in the group. As Bolan had expected, the man's finger curled reflexively on the trigger of his Steyr MPi69. A volley of 9 mm rounds stitched a corkscrew pattern up the front of the man in the opposite corner, blowing out his intestines and lungs.

The lantern struck one of the forward gunners on the shoulder, overturning and bursting into flames as the kerosene ignited. The gunman screamed, the flames licking up his shirt and flesh, casting the only light inside the shed now. His partner turned, trying to beat out the flames with his coat as Reinmaul screamed orders to the man that he should forget his comrade and concentrate on Bolan.

The Executioner's fist slammed into the youngest gunman's jaw, his left hand shoving the Steyr downward. Bolan followed up with an elbow, knocking his adversary's head against the side of the shed. His opponent's eyes rolled up into his head as he slumped to the floor, and his grip relaxed on the Steyr.

Bolan grabbed the weapon and swung the muzzle in the direction of his confused enemy. The first controlled burst caught the burning gunman in the side, punching holes through his chest. The rounds jolted the man, spinning him into his partner, who was still trying to recover from the shock.

Reinmaul maneuvered around the pair, bursting through the exit and running for the car. The remaining hardman disentangled himself from the rag-doll form of his partner. He tipped the Steyr's muzzle in Bolan's direction, but the veteran warrior was too fast. Bolan fired another burst, his Steyr chattering as the 9 mm slugs struck home. The gunman collapsed to the floor as his weapon sputtered uselessly, its rounds gouging wood slivers out of the ceiling.

The kerosene lamp had set the floor on fire, and the flames began to spread quickly up the wall where Reinmaul had stood. Bolan spun and grabbed a handful of the unconscious hardman's shirt, dragging him from the shed through the choking haze and smoke of burning wood. Tears flooded the soldier's eyes, and he released the thug's shirt, leaving him to lie on the ground.

Bolan sprinted toward the vehicle, the Steyr clutched in his fist at high ready. He arrived to the sound of a starting engine, and he stopped short, firing the Steyr as he raised it in a two-handed grip. Slugs whined off the BMW as Reinmaul swung the sedan into the clearing. The engine roared in protest as she stromped the accelerator. Bolan continued to fire, but his weapon seemed to have no effect—the car was reinforced with armor.

As the taillights of the sedan faded into the distance, Bolan cursed.

He turned and made his way back to the shed, which was now fully engulfed in flames. Any evidence he might have had was burning. Within the hour, there would only be ashes. Bolan turned his attention to the young soldier, now regaining consciousness. He forced the young man to his feet, pushing him in the direction of the path. The youth stumbled several steps before falling. Bolan grabbed him by the shirt collar, hauling him to his feet again.

When they had traversed the path to the clearing, Bolan ordered his prisoner to sit on the grass. He studied the fresh-faced youth in the light of the full harvest moon. The young man met Bolan's piercing gaze for a moment, then lowered his head. He couldn't have been more than eighteen or nineteen, with blond hair and the faintest hint of a mustache. He was out of breath, and Bolan could make out the large welt his blows had left, even in the semidarkness.

The soldier trained the muzzle of the Steyr on an imaginary point between the youth's eyes, careful to keep the barrel just out of reach.

"You want to tell me who you are and what the hell is going on?"

"I tell you nothing, American!" he said with a sneer, then he spit on the toe of Bolan's boot, but the Executioner was unmoved by the gesture.

"You sure about that?" he asked. "If you don't want to talk, I have no reason to keep you alive."

"Then kill me!" the youth challenged. "I die with honor."

Bolan scowled at the young man, something flashing in his eyes that warned he would make good on his threat. "Do you think there's any honor in this?" the soldier asked.

The youth remained silent.

"Do you think there's any honor in terrorizing innocent people? In working for scum like Schleyer and Linger?

That's not being a soldier. It's called murder. It's called terrorism, and it's the kind people can't tolerate. Now, you can do yourself a favor and talk to me, and I let you take your chances with the police. Or I can kill you now. Sure, either way you lose. But it's up to you whether you want to lose alive or lose dead."

The young man studied Bolan, the hatred in his eyes replaced with fear. Bolan was getting to him.

"You're young," Bolan added more quietly. "You've got your whole life ahead of you. Don't throw it away now for people who don't give a damn about you. Do you honestly think that if you go back and report failure that they'll let you live? I know what kind of man Dortmund Linger is. So do you. He'll kill you in a heartbeat. Don't toss your life away for that scum. Talk to me."

"They are building a plane," the youth said quietly. Tears filled the young man's eyes, and his voice shook as he spoke. "They are going to use it against your country."

"How?" Bolan demanded.

"I do not know," the German lad replied, shaking his head. "I know they are on a tight schedule. We are working many hours...working to get done on time."

"Who set me up? Gabi?"

The youth nodded. "She had orders. We were to ambush you, try to take you alive."

"Alive? Why? Who ordered I be taken alive?"

"Commander Linger. He want to know about you." The youth struggled to make himself understood. "Want to know who you are. What you are doing in Frankfurt, *verstehen?*"

"Yeah, I understand," the Executioner replied, his thoughts in turmoil now. "What about Edel Schleyer? Is he working with Linger?"

"I know no Schleyer. Only Commander Linger. I am under Lieutenant Einsbaum."

"Who is this Einsbaum?"

The youth nodded in the direction of the crackling flames that were rapidly consuming the wooden shed. "He is dead. He died hero."

"He died stupid," Bolan countered. "What about this plane? When are they scheduled to finish it?"

"I do not know."

"Then what exactly is their plan? How are they going to use one plane against a whole country?"

"I do not know."

"Don't lie to me," Bolan warned. "It won't help your cause any."

"I swear, American. I only help to build, follow orders as good soldier. That is all I know."

"Is Dr. Krizova being forced to help Linger?"

"*Ja,* they force him to work. They say they will kill his *kinder.* He is a Czech, but very smart."

"I know who he is," Bolan snapped. "Where is it? Tell me where they are building the plane."

The German youth hesitated at first, and Bolan waved the Steyr to emphasize he expected an answer. The youth had slipped up, and both of them knew it. By disclosing his involvement in the construction, he would have to know the location of the plane.

"A secret tunnel," the youth finally confessed. "Out of the zug, the train. Deserted tunnel leads to hangar. This is where plane is."

"Which station?"

"Tanusenlage."

"All right, get out of here," Bolan said, hearing the two-tone siren of the police wailing in the night.

"What?"

"I said to get the hell out of here. Before I change my mind." He waved the Steyr toward the nearby road. "Go!"

The youth was frightened at first, rising to a crouch and

sizing up Bolan. He was afraid that in his flight, his enemy would shoot him in the back. Bolan waited, wary the German might try to take him. Finally, the young man spun and ran toward the road, tripping twice on wooded ground before disappearing into the darkness.

Bolan popped the clip of his weapon, which was half-empty. He turned and began to traverse the woods parallel to the road, using it and the river to guide him. He headed back in the direction of the bridge Reinmaul had crossed earlier that evening, stopping twice within a two-minute interval and checking a small compass on his wristwatch. If he continued on his course, he could make the hotel in just under an hour.

A light rain began to fall, and Bolan considered the situation as he hurried through the pitch-black woods. He considered what the German youth had told him about Linger's plans to build the jet. A fully functional prototype in the wrong hands would have devastating results. And the enemy wanted to use the aircraft against the U.S. Failure to destroy Linger's army could prove catastrophic.

If worse came to worst, he'd have to destroy the let.

The other half of the problem concerned Krizova. The scientist was Bolan's true mission. He would be forced to remove Krizova from the line of fire, so any action had to be preceded by a soft probe on the hangar.

Then there was the issue of fresh weaponry, and Bolan wished he had Kissinger on hand to help in that department. For the moment, he had only the Beretta with an extra clip, the Desert Eagle and the Steyr. Everything else in his arsenal had gone up with the Aries, including his demolition bag. He was left in enemy territory, clearly outgunned, and he couldn't help but wonder if the enemy had the upper hand right at the moment.

Undoubtedly, Bolan knew he was also wanted by the police, and Kaufmann had been quite clear on how the

BND felt about him. He wasn't going to worry. Worry was a soldier's worst enemy, even when the chips were down and the odds stacked so high he couldn't see over them. The Executioner would just have to make do with what he had, and plan carefully for every eventuality.

As Bolan continued his journey, the darkness seemed to close in on him.

JÜTTA KAUFMANN STRAINED to see through the rain and mud-washed windshield of her car as she maneuvered through the narrow city streets. The sky was ominously dark, interspersed with lightning, and rain hammered the city streets with intensity. She couldn't push Baldric Gerhard's information from her mind. It could well be true the American government was sending someone to help Belasko.

The only question was how Gerhard really came by that information.

She had known Gerhard for many years, but that didn't mean she completely trusted him. It was sad to think people involved with the nation's internal security weren't trustworthy. Kaufmann didn't consider her skepticism unreasonable. She and Belasko had been encountered at every turn. She also had to believe that Linger probably still had sympathizers or friends inside the BND.

Kaufmann had begun her law-enforcement career early, entering the Berlin police academy after graduating from the University of Frankfurt. Her academy days were filled with inflated standards, unfair treatment and unbelievable prejudices. Nevertheless, she persisted and soon graduated with honors. She began working a foot beat in Berlin, then transferred to Frankfurt after the collapse of the Berlin Wall.

It was in Frankfurt that Kaufmann met Fredric, a watchmaker and Swiss entrepreneur. Sadly, his marriage to her left him feeling unsatisfied, unable to shake his two favorite things—the bottle and women. Her brief marriage ended as a result of a double shooting that involved the death of her partner, a fine German man with whom Kaufmann had been having an affair. The facts of their relationship came out during the board of inquiry investigation.

Shortly after returning to duty, she was approached by Dortmund Linger, a recently promoted officer in the BND who had seemed to take an interest in her impeccable record with the police. She jumped at the opportunity to serve with the organization. The BND's responsibilities were similar to the those of the American NSA and Secret Service combined. They protected the chancellor, investigated intergovernmental fraud and criminal activities by major federal organizations and enforced political laws.

The BND's power wasn't limited to Germany, although downsizing of their counterespionage division had been in the natural order of things. Kaufmann served in numerous positions with honor, finally achieving the rank of internal-security agent. Her credentials spoke for themselves. She was a crack shot, an expert in unarmed combat and maintained good physical fitness and a spotless service record.

Her assignment to find and eliminate Dortmund Linger hadn't been an easy one. Much of her career had been spent in pursuit of the elusive mercenary. She had decided not to tell Belasko of her close ties with Linger. In some ways, it was ironic, as if Linger had been training a replacement, not mentoring a promising young woman. Now the hunter had become the hunted, and Jütta Kaufmann had to put her personal feelings aside after seeing Linger's handiwork. She no longer admired Linger. She pitied him, actually. He was a dangerous criminal who had to be stopped, a man who threatened the very security of her country and its people.

Dortmund Linger was a traitor to Germany, and Kaufmann meant to right that wrong.

A pair of headlights swung in behind her car as Kaufmann turned onto the entry ramp of the autobahn. It didn't necessarily mean anything, but she couldn't afford to take chances at this stage of the game. If it was a tail, she needed to establish intelligence before she could act. She checked her watch. If the government agent from America was scheduled to arrive posing as a Lufthansa pilot, Kaufmann would have her work cut out for her.

Moreover, if the car behind her posed a real threat, that threat would carry on to Belasko's contact. She was going to have to deal with this more immediate problem if she was to find the American agent successfully.

Kaufmann hoped Herr Joseph Grimes wouldn't get caught in the cross fire.

JACK GRIMALDI SQUINTED at the dark, stormy weather through the cockpit of Lufthansa Flight 808 from Washington, D.C., to Frankfurt. The inclement weather had caused delays too numerous to count, and he was finally given permission to land after nearly an hour in a holding pattern. The lights of the runway were barely visible as Grimaldi descended on his final approach.

It seemed as if nothing had gone right with his trip from the beginning.

Barbara Price had his uniform, credentials and all arrangements made upon his arrival at Dulles International Airport. The brief he received had been just that—brief. But none of it mattered when he heard that Striker could be in trouble. That was his cue, and Jack Grimaldi held no quarter where his friend was concerned. Mack Bolan had saved Grimaldi's life way too many times for him to grumble about a few petty inconveniences.

If Bolan was in trouble, then Jack Grimaldi was there. End of story.

Grimaldi smiled at the thought of the unmarked container in the baggage compartment. Stony Man's connections were far and wide. Slipping a stash of weapons in under the noses of American officials was easy. Getting them off the plane and safely into Grimaldi's hands would be another story. German policy was that all baggage went through customs, and German customs officials were known to be tenacious in their duties. Grimaldi would just have to improvise.

The immediate concern was setting down the huge Boeing 757 intact. A piece of cake for a man like Jack Grimaldi. The ace pilot's career had begun with gunships in Vietnam. It should have been easy for Grimaldi to make an honest living after returning stateside, but the appeal of hard cash held the glamour for him, and the Mafia seemed to have the most of it.

But one fateful night in Las Vegas changed all that, when Jack Grimaldi came face to face with the Executioner.

Grimaldi's soul had been literally converted by Bolan's private war, and he could understand his friend's passions. Grimaldi signed on with Bolan to become a permanent part of whatever cause took his liking, and he had never looked back. The two men had been through practically everything imaginable—enough to fill several lifetimes.

With Stony Man having no word from Bolan in almost two days, and the clock ticking, Grimaldi didn't hesitate to fly out immediately. So far, his cover seemed good. Lufthansa pilots were required to be bilingual, but Grimaldi's English could hardly pass a modest test, let alone throwing a whole new language into it. Fortunately, the copilot and navigator were also Americans, and two of the five flight attendants who were German spoke excellent English.

Grimaldi considered the mission ahead with resolute

skepticism. He had less than forty-eight hours to find Bolan. Price indicated there were contacts with both the CIA and BND who could help, but he had no idea who or where. It was just another situation he'd have to play by ear.

The Stony Man Pilot set the Boeing on the runway with a picture-perfect landing, and taxied the plane toward a reserved spot near the terminal. The storm had caused unscheduled landings of planes bound for parts unknown, and Grimaldi could already see his crew and passengers were in for one wet off-loading. As the plane rolled to a halt, he began to shut down all systems. The copilot agreed to see the passengers out at his request, and the navigator deplaned to file their flight logs.

Grimaldi was left alone in the cockpit. As he continued to disengage the controls, a flash caught the corner of his eye. He leaned forward in his seat and noticed a black BMW pull up on the tarmac, and two men in long black trench coats exited from the rear. He couldn't make out their faces, but the expressions were unmistakable. They took up an attitude of expectancy and official authority. Were they waiting for him? Could his cover have been compromised so quickly?

He stood, bent slightly in the cramped cockpit and slid into his uniform overcoat. He pulled his satchel from under the seat and headed to the front. The disembarkation was still in progress, and Grimaldi inserted himself into the crowd. He was unsure if he could blend in with the uniform, but he had to give it his best shot. The going was slow, and the mysterious observers would easily be able to scan every face in the crowd.

As Grimaldi reached the bottom of the steps, a customs official in full uniform stepped up from nowhere and gave the pilot a curt nod.

"Herr Grimes?" the man snapped. *"Guten abend. Ich bin Zollamt Offizier Krüger. Kommen Sie bitte um einst."*

"Huh?" Grimaldi replied.

The man spun on his heel and Grimaldi figured he was being asked to follow. He fell into step, the sound of his heart pulsing in his ears. Grimaldi clenched his one free hand, willing himself to be calm. The customs officer led him around the nose of the plane to where the baggage was being unloaded. The large crate was off to the side of the motor-controlled ramp, and Grimaldi's stomach leaped into his throat.

The officer pointed dutifully to the crate. *"Machen Sie es auf."*

"I'm sorry, what did you say?" Grimaldi said, shaking his head with confusion.

"Open this please."

"Why? That thing doesn't belong to me," Grimaldi protested.

Before the officer could reply, the two men from the BMW approached. Grimaldi silently wished he were armed, but he couldn't let on that he knew anything about the crate. He had known the reputation of German customs officials, but he hadn't been prepared for such a confrontation as he was now faced with. The most troubling part was that nobody should have known the crate was even his. The two men flashed their credentials so quickly, Grimaldi didn't have time to make them out. The rain had stopped now, but the bitter wind seemed to bite Grimaldi's skin right through the thin uniform material.

"Are you saying that this crate does not belong to you, Herr Grimes?" one of the trench-coated men said.

"Yeah, that's what I'm saying."

"Das ist his Gepäck," a woman's voice said from behind him.

All eyes turned toward a beautiful brunette holding up her own credentials, and Grimaldi was really confused now. Everybody seemed to be more interested in the crate than in Grimaldi, and he still didn't have a clue as to who the hell any of these people were or what they wanted.

"Sir," Jütta Kaufmann announced, "you are under arrest."

9

The customs officer and the two mysterious men looked at the woman in silence, the shock evident on their faces.

Jack Grimaldi wasn't sure what to do next, but something in his gut told him to trust the dark-haired beauty over her three male counterparts. From where Grimaldi stood, it was obvious this was a tense moment of interagency conflict. He decided to listen to his instincts and turned to face the woman.

"Under arrest for what?" Grimaldi asked. "I haven't done anything."

"Herr Grimes, do not act so coy," she replied. "I am Jütta Kaufmann, an agent for the BND. I know you have smuggled weapons into this country, and I believe you are selling them to known terrorists. Therefore, this incident falls under the authority of the BND, as it is a threat to the internal security of the Federal Republic of Germany. Now, turn around please and put your hands on your head."

A heated discussion followed as Grimaldi complied, setting down the attaché case in his right hand. The customs officer remained silent, but the two men began to argue with her. They bantered back and forth for several minutes as Kaufmann patted down Grimaldi. It was too weird. The BND agent seemed to know the crate was filled with weapons. That meant Barbara Price's contact within the BND had painted Grimaldi as a criminal. Grimaldi was guessing the President's wishes had been disregarded. It also meant they knew he was there to help Bolan. Grimaldi could only conclude Stony Man had a traitor in the midst of its German connections.

As Kaufmann's hand passed his right coat pocket, Grimaldi felt something cold and hard slide through the waistband of his uniform pants at the small of his back. It was a gun! She had planted a gun on him, and Grimaldi couldn't understand why she was trying to pin him with it. There was no way he could have boarded the plane in the States with a gun—nobody would believe he was armed now. In the next moment, her reason became obvious.

The BND agent's arm snaked past his shoulder, an HK4 pistol clutched in her fist. She squeezed the trigger at point-blank range to the closer of the trench-coated pair. Grimaldi's mouth dropped open a half second after the 9 mm round cored through the man's head, blood and brain matter showering his partner and the customs officer. Kaufmann swung her pistol in the direction of the second man as the customs officer staggered backward. The officer clawed at his holster, but Grimaldi had whipped out his newly acquired Heckler & Koch P-7 pistol and pointed it at the customs man. The officer raised his hands in surrender.

The other man wasn't as smart. He dived to the rain-soaked tarmac, rolling away from their position and digging in his coat for his own gun. The man produced an Uzi machine pistol a second too late. Kaufmann fired twice more, the first round catching the man's wrist, the second tearing out his throat. She ran forward and kicked the weapon away from the gunman's grip, then lifted the ID wallets from both dead men.

"Let's go!" she yelled at Grimaldi.

The pilot didn't have to be told twice. He grabbed the attaché case while Kaufmann relieved the customs officer of his weapon. Grimaldi followed her as she raced away from the plane. He could hear the fading sound of a high-pitched whistle, followed by many pairs of leather boots slapping pavement.

"Where the hell are we going?" Grimaldi shouted, struggling to keep up with his lithe ally.

"No time!" Kaufmann called. "You will have to trust me!"

"Whatever," Grimaldi retorted breathlessly.

They quickly reached Kaufmann's car, Grimaldi taking the passenger's side as the woman slid behind the wheel. Within seconds, she had the car in motion, turning a tight circle and making a beeline for a distant gate. Grimaldi could barely make out shouts behind them and the sound of autofire as they tore through the open gate. Kaufmann struggled to keep her vehicle under control as she jerked the wheel in a hard left, maneuvering onto a gravel road. They descended a hill, and the lights of the airport disappeared from view.

Grimaldi checked the rear window several more times before finally blowing out a gust of relief through pursed lips. He turned and studied his rescuer for a moment. Grimaldi could hardly fathom what had just happened, but he wasn't about to trust anybody. He tucked the customs official's pistol in his belt and trained the P-7 on the woman.

"I'm sorry," Grimaldi muttered, "but until I have some answers, I can't trust you. I can't trust anybody."

Kaufmann turned to see the pistol pointed at her. She scowled at first, then the look was replaced by a smile and she chuckled softly. She shook her head as she studied the winding road in front of them.

"What's so funny?" Grimaldi asked.

"You Americans are funny," she retorted. She turned to look at him again, adding, "You can put your weapon away. I am here to help you."

"Can you prove that?"

"Did I not just save your life back at the airport?" she asked defensively.

"That doesn't mean anything. You might have your own agenda for me."

Kaufmann laughed again. "Yes, you are truly a friend of Mike Belasko."

"Who?" Grimaldi replied, trying not to reveal his surprise.

"I am on his side," the woman remarked. She fixed him with an icy stare. "And yours, unless you do not put your weapon away."

Grimaldi hesitated a moment before nodding and lowering the pistol. "I'm sorry, but I had strict instructions not to trust anyone."

"Your people should take their own advice."

"What do mean?"

Kaufmann let out a frustrated sigh. "Someone from your government has been feeding intelligence to people within my command. That is why these problems have arisen. Those same people are working for the enemy. This entire operation was an attempt to kill both of us. I knew this, but you did not."

"Why would the German customs officials be involved in affairs of political espionage?" he queried.

"They are not involved." Kaufmann reached into her jacket pocket and withdrew the two ID wallets. "These credentials are simple forgeries. Those men are not police—they are part of Dortmund Linger's private army."

Grimaldi nodded, jerking his thumb to the attaché case in the back seat. "That has information meant for Belasko. We figured this Linger as a principal player. My people have apparently found a link between Linger and Krizova, and they wanted Belasko to have every advantage. For some reason, communications have broken down. He was supposed to contact us only through official channels, but the CIA claims they have no word from him.''

''That is not right,'' Kaufmann rebutted. ''Mike told me he spoke with Dan Lincoln, a case chief with the CIA office here in Frankfurt.''

''Then somebody really has their wires crossed, because we haven't heard a word. I guess your bosses are on the warpath, as well. We have it on the best sources the BND has a 'shoot-to-kill' policy regarding Belasko.'' Grimaldi's voice was grim. ''We have less than forty-eight hours to find him.''

''I was implicated in this,'' Kaufmann stated with a nod. ''My own people are watching me, and they know I have been in contact with your friend. Herr Lincoln arranged for a meet with a contact. A woman who was going to supply weapons and information. I told him it was a trap, but he would not listen.''

Grimaldi smiled. ''No, he usually doesn't. He follows his own agenda.''

''We must find him,'' she said, ''but I must first check into something. Will you come with me?''

''Sure, I guess. I mean, I owe you at least that much. But what about those weapons? We can't just leave them in the hands of the customs people.''

''We might be able to help each other. I know how to get them back. Right now, I must look at something. It is important for both the German people and the Americans.''

''Drive on, lady,'' Grimaldi commented.

BOLAN RETURNED to the hotel and discovered that Kaufmann had left. There were no notes, but Bolan recalled her mentioning a meeting with a supervisor. He checked his watch. It was now past midnight, and the clock was ticking. He didn't have time to wait for her. It was better off that way. He was accustomed to working alone, and there was no point in worrying about her. Kaufmann could take care of herself.

The soldier showered to wash away the stench of smoke and sweat, then donned his combat blacksuit, counting himself lucky to have had enough foresight to pull a box of 9 mm Parabellum rounds from the trunk and store it in his room earlier that day. At least he wouldn't be as radically outgunned as he had first surmised. He quickly loaded a spare clip for the Beretta, then stripped the Desert Eagle and wiped it down. Without a light oiling, he hoped the weapon wouldn't malfunction after its exposure to the weather.

Bolan reloaded the Steyr, then slung the weapon barrel to hang under his right arm. That accomplished, he shrugged into his long overcoat and headed out. The train ride to the district of Tanusenlage was quick, and within ten minutes, he found the deserted tunnel entrance. Checking the platform to ensure no one was watching, he then leaped the electronic gate that closed off the old tunnel. He ditched the overcoat and moved into the darkness.

He crouched, letting his eyes adjust before continuing. The tunnel took a sharp right and descended, and Bolan used his palm against the wall as a guide. The trek was slow, each step unsure as the surroundings became darker. The faint sound of dripping water could be heard intermittently, and Bolan figured he was near streets at those times. Probably the water that passed through curb grates and into the storm sewers.

The air in the train tunnel was cold and damp. Occasionally, he would stop to listen, but only the sounds of rats and the water were audible. He wondered if the young mercenary had even told the truth. The whole thing could have been bogus, a quick way to throw the Executioner off the scent. Something deep down told him the kid hadn't lied.

Twenty minutes elapsed…thirty…forty. Bolan had been negotiating the tunnel almost an hour when his next stop to listen was rewarded with different sounds—sounds of machinery, men's voices and work being done. There was also the faintest humming sound, which seemed to emanate from the walls. Generators, probably providing electricity—maybe a boiler as well.

Bolan proceeded with caution. It appeared to be getting lighter. The wall gave way to space, and the soldier realized it was a branch off the main tunnel. He stopped to listen again, then turned and crept along the side tunnel. He could reach out to touch the walls on both sides, and the ground under his feet was no longer uneven. He crouched to feel the floor. Cold and rough metal pressed against his palm. It was a gratelike flooring. He was in some kind of walkway. Bolan continued until a door appeared directly in his path.

The Executioner turned the handle but the door would not swing in or out, perhaps due to a dead bolt or just rust from years of disuse. He unholstered his Beretta and pushed his weight against the door. The first two attempts did nothing, but then it gave in on the third try. Bolan wedged his way into the opening, shading his eyes against the sudden light spilling through a window in one wall.

The soldier stood in an empty cubicle, about twenty-five-feet square. The stone and rock of the tunnel had been replaced by thin metal, and the floor was made of the same grate material. A trapdoor with a handle mounted in the flooring descended to the level below. Bolan padded silently to the window and peered through it.

There it was. The sleek plane sat in the middle of a huge hangar literally cut from the rock. Men moved busily around the fighter's exterior, flanked by a score of armed soldiers. Many of the armed guards appeared to be working, as well, moving bulky crates of equipment or assisting as technicians soldered and welded. Treacherously high scaffolding was networked around the plane like the web of a spider. The German youth hadn't been lying. The fighter appeared near completion.

A small man in a white lab coat stood near a table at the front of the plane, directing work on the cockpit section. Based on Stony Man's description, it had to be Vasec Krizova. Bolan studied the work force a minute longer, checking positions, probable fields of fire and sheer numbers. He counted twenty-six armed soldiers, more than three-quarters assigned to various work details. The hangar itself was circular, well lit and had what appeared to be several smaller branches other than what he presumed was a launching tunnel.

Bolan edged away from the window and considered his options. He was obviously in some kind of watchtower. Why there was no sentry posted here was a mystery, but he counted himself fortunate. Without demolitions, blowing the launch tunnel was out of the question. He would have to find some other way to sabotage the operation.

The sound of screeching metal caught his attention. Bolan spun to see the trapdoor swinging up toward him. He thumbed the selector switch to single bursts and crouched against the wall. The soldier trained his pistol sights over the top of the door. The back of the new arrival's head appeared, followed by shoulders as he ascended the ladder well. Bolan stepped forward and drove the butt of his Beretta behind the man's ear. The mercenary groaned, slumping forward. The soldier hauled the unconscious man the rest of the way through the door, then pointed the Beretta down the ladder well.

The guard was alone.

Bolan used the sling on the Steyr MPi69 to gag the man, and the belt of his uniform pants to tie his hands and feet behind him. He checked to ensure the man was breathing, then stripped him of a Ka-bar fighting knife, two fragmentation grenades and the clip from his weapon. He dragged the man through the small opening in the door, leaving him in the tunnel. Nobody would hear the guard when he came to, and anyone checking the tower would simply think it was abandoned.

In any case, it would buy the Executioner some time to move on with the mission.

Bolan holstered his pistol and quickly descended the ladder. When he reached bottom, he crouched and swung up the Steyr. He needed to conduct a soft probe, make sure he knew the odds before formulating a plan. It stood to reason there were explosives somewhere inside the hangar. Finding them would be another story, coupled with the fact he needed to devise a way to get Krizova out of harm's way.

The soldier inched forward, peering around the corner of his small cover. Moving through the hangar area undetected would be impossible. He now had a fairly good view of the starboard side of the aircraft, with the tail fins almost directly ahead. The huge jet would provide him with some shadows. Bolan moved along the wall cautiously, sweeping the Steyr in preparation for any opposition.

An armed guard near the front landing gear looked over in his direction. The man called an alarm, swinging his Uzi toward Bolan's position. The Executioner triggered the Steyr, his first three rounds taking the soldier high in the chest. The man flew backward, his head contacting the table before he fell to the ground.

Time for a tactical retreat.

Shouts of alarm went up everywhere, and Bolan cursed the fact his luck hadn't held. The Executioner rose to his full height and sprinted behind the back of the fighter, using it to shield himself from a fresh onslaught of gunfire. He could hear one man screaming to be careful of the fighter, and the firing ceased. Bolan noted the entryway on his right flank. He palmed one of the frag grenades releasing the spoon as he sprinted for the entryway. He lobbed the grenade into the midst of a group of mercs rushing him on the left.

The bomb exploded with thunderous effect before touching the ground. Shrapnel tore at tender flesh as the concussion cracked the skulls of two soldiers closest to the blast. Chaos and panic overtook the gunmen, and one officer was yelling orders. Bolan triggered his weapon again, the rounds shattering the officer's jaw even as he was still screaming.

Gunfire erupted once again, stitching ugly patterns in the wall just behind Bolan. If anything, Linger's men didn't understand the concept of leading a target. He reached the entryway, crashing into another unsuspecting merc coming through the doorway to investigate the commotion. Bolan drove the butt of his Steyr into the man's gut, the air leaving his opponent's lungs as he doubled over from the blow. Bolan followed up with an elbow to the man's neck, the crack of vertebrae audible above the scattered gunfire.

Bolan burst through the door and sprinted down a poorly lit hallway. He had almost reached a far T-intersection when two guards rounded the corner. The Executioner was firing before either merc could bring a weapon to bear. As the close-range shots slammed the men against the wall, Bolan rounded the corner.

Dead end! Bolan changed directions, moving past the intersection as his pursuers charged down the branching corridor. A standoff in narrow confines against so many guns was tantamount to suicide. The soldier continued, bearing left and right as the corridor wound through the underground complex. Another left brought him up short against a wooden door, which was locked. He applied a well-placed kick, sending the door crashing inward, and discovered he was back in the hangar, the front of the fighter now in view straight ahead of him.

Bolan tore off to the right, firing on two sentries near a second door almost directly across from his original entry site. The guards dived away, one taking a round in the neck and shoulder while his comrade managed to avoid being hit. The Executioner dropped and rolled as the uninjured merc triggered his Steyr. Rounds sizzled overhead as Bolan targeted from his new position. This time, he didn't miss. A half-dozen Parabellum rounds drilled into the target's head and shoulders.

The Executioner made the unguarded door, his dogged pursuers close behind. He pushed through the door and found himself in a wide room filled with equipment. Boxes and crates were stacked floor to ceiling, creating a literal maze. Bolan pressed on, weaving his way through the storage room to finally access a door on the far side. He pressed his ear against a panel, then tried the handle. The door opened smoothly, and he entered in a crouch.

The familiar clacking of gun bolts slamming home assaulted his ears, and he found himself staring at a dozen Uzi and Steyr muzzles. A big blond man in a black leather coat and fatigue pants stood among the group of mercenaries, an evil smile pasted on his face, studying Bolan with mock satisfaction.

Bolan considered his options, but quickly realized they had him cold.

He set the Steyr on the ground in front of him and raised his hands. The blond man casually reached down and relieved him of his weapons. He handed them to a nearby aide, then put his hands on his hips, the grin widening as he sized up his nemesis. Bolan returned the stare with equal challenge.

"Welcome, Herr Belasko," Dortmund Linger said. "We've been expecting you."

10

Mack Bolan stared challengingly at Linger.

If the former BND agent wanted him dead, he could have killed Bolan right there. What the Executioner couldn't understand was the ambush at the shed by Gabi Reinmaul's people. Linger's statement betrayed the truth of Bolan's situation; they *had* been waiting for him. Undoubtedly, Reinmaul had told them of his escape, and they probably surmised one of their people would give up the location of the secret underground tunnel.

Linger ordered Bolan's hands tied behind him and had him blindfolded. The merc leader then directed six men to be an escort, and the rest to return to their duties. Bolan felt himself led along a corridor. The air became increasingly cool, and he could feel the sharp descent as they went deeper underground.

The group finally stopped, and Bolan could hear the opening of a heavy metal door. Linger ordered his men to tie the prisoner's feet and strip him down. That accomplished, the soldier could feel the chill of the room, and he almost wondered if the increased cold was due to their depth underground or if was being held in some kind of walk-in freezer.

In the pitch dark caused by the blindfold, Bolan was unprepared for his arms to be yanked up over his head. His feet left the floor, and the shock of the sudden jerking motion almost took his breath away, so did the ice-cold water thrown on his naked form as he dangled freely. The water had a quick effect when combined with the chilly air surrounding Bolan. He began to shiver, already feeling his body temperature drop as the evaporating water cooled him rapidly.

The Executioner was familiar with the technique. He knew it was just one of the many ordeals he would endure at the hands of his captors. Men like Linger were perpetual artists at torture. Bolan had run into many of his kind over the years, starting with the officers at POW camps in Vietnam, and through his wars against the Mafia, KGB and terrorists.

In some strange way, Bolan considered another angle while hanging there and shivering to keep warm. Torturing him didn't make any sense, unless they wanted to do it for the purpose of extracting information. Otherwise, torture was nothing more than a method of exacting revenge and punishment for his interference in their plans. Linger was a soldier, and Bolan didn't believe he was into inflicting pain just for some sadistic thrill. Torture had to have a purpose in a soldier's mind.

Bolan was aware of the use of scopolamine on people in the past by Stony Man's Phoenix Force. There had even been a couple of deaths as a result of its use. Bolan didn't personally agree with such techniques; he believed in a more direct route of obtaining information. Nevertheless, he understood the necessity of such things in war. And that was what Linger obviously considered the present situation. All of this began to lead Bolan to conclude someone else was running the show.

Bolan was guessing the man in charge was Edel Schleyer.

Linger's voice intruded on Bolan's train of thought. ''Well, Herr Belasko. I don't suppose you'd care to tell me what exactly it was you were hoping to accomplish by coming here?''

"Not really," Bolan replied, trying to control the shaking. He willed his muscles to relax, but it seemed almost impossible. The more he tried, the more he shook.

Bolan remembered something the military had taught him many years before. He could hear the words of his drill sergeant coming back to him, echoing in his mind. "Cold and sleep deprivation are two of the most effective methods the enemy can use to make you talk. There is nothing more humiliating, because depriving a man of sleep or body temperature prevents him from doing even the most basic things, like counting objects or remembering specific details about their past history."

"Why don't you make this easy on yourself?" Linger hissed. "Just tell us who you really are, and what you are doing here, and I will kill you quickly. You will die with honor, like a real soldier."

"Is that right?" Bolan asked, actually managing a laugh. It felt as if the cold were sucking the very life out of him. "Tell me something, Commander Linger, who is 'us'? Who's really pushing the buttons on this operation?"

"You know who I am," Linger replied. "I guess that Jütta Kaufmann has been talking about me."

Bolan tensed slightly at the mention of her name. "What the hell are you talking about?"

"Oh, come now, Herr Belasko. Let's not toy with each other. Do you honestly think I don't know that you have been secretly working with her to find me? Now that you have found me, what is it you intend to do to me, eh? Did you think that I would just roll over and show you my belly like a dog?

"I am a professional soldier, just like you. I have seen you in action. I do not believe you work for the American CIA. And just like you," Linger continued with emphasis,

"I find excitement from the hunt, the stench of gunfire and death."

"The only problem with you, Linger," Bolan interjected through gritted teeth, "is that excitement is usually from the death of innocent people after you've mowed them down."

"I am a warrior. We are not as different as you pretend."

"We're a lot different, Linger," Bolan snapped. "You murder innocent people."

"Enough idle talk!" Linger ordered. "I want to know who you are really working for. What are you doing here? Were you hoping to sabotage the plane? What do you know of our plans?"

"Go to hell."

There was a brief silence before the air was literally forced from Bolan's gut. He wasn't prepared for the fist that connected with his abdomen like a sledgehammer. Air whooshed from his lungs, and it felt as if his chest were on fire. Bolan took several gasping breaths before his regular breathing effort returned. The ropes tying his hands chafed his wrists as he swung and spun on whatever was holding him off the ground. The air cooled his body more, and the effect of spinning in the darkness was disorienting.

"Do not toy with me, Herr Belasko," Linger warned. "I am in no mood to play games with you. If you do not answer my questions, I will kill you, and it will be the most slow and painful death you can ever imagine."

"Go to hell," Bolan repeated, gritting his teeth.

He took another blow to the gut, but he had readied himself for this one, tightening his lean stomach muscles. He wouldn't be able to resist those kinds of blows for long. He would make his best attempt not to cave in. Bolan knew his limitations, and he'd been pushed there before. Some had pushed him beyond the breaking point, but the Executioner had always come through it with a few more scars.

For a man to think he would never talk, no matter what he had to endure, was complete and utter nonsense. Everyone had a breaking point, and a real specialist in the craft could always find out where that point was. Half of torture involved the psychological aspects, because some had an extremely high tolerance to pain. Bolan's experience and training would help him to resist, but he wasn't sure for how long. One thing was certain. It would take more than a few punches to the stomach.

Another bucket of ice water hit Bolan, followed by a third and fourth blow to his gut while he took in a sudden breath, leaving him off guard. Pain racked his brain like pool balls during an opening break. Stars danced in front of his eyes, and the pressure from the blindfold seemed to increase. Spasms and twinges of pain rippled through his abdomen. Bolan ground his teeth, fighting back the urge to scream.

The shivering began once more, and he fought to remain conscious. He could hear men laughing at him as he swung freely. The motion was really starting to bother him. Taking such blows while still was one thing, but every set of punches sent him swinging to and fro, the ropes spinning him like a phone cord.

"Are you going to talk to me now?" Linger asked.

The mercenary's words seemed to move slowly, like a recording played at low speed, and Bolan found it difficult to comprehend what was being asked.

"Do you think I like to do this?" Linger mocked. "I am a busy man. I do not have time to be worried about what you are doing to stop the cause. My associate has other ideas. I don't really care." Bolan could sense Linger move closer, his voice barely a whisper. "My men are loyal to me. The Iron Skull answers to no one. We are only doing this to further our own cause. Our vision is simple. We want to be as rich as possible. So you can see, we are of one singularity. Our job is to protect that which we cherish most—money."

Soft laughter could be heard in the background, and Bolan sensed they weren't alone in the room. He tried to focus on how many distinctively different voices there were, but it was becoming more difficult to concentrate. Bolan was very cold now. He was sure there were at least…three? Had the rest gone away? It wasn't as if Bolan could escape now. Another punch to the gut came, probably for his failure to answer Linger.

With that blow, the darkness folded in around Mack Bolan.

JÜTTA KAUFMANN SWORE softly in German as she peered through the special night-vision binoculars. Off in the distance, she could make out the fortress of Edel Schleyer. Armed sentries roamed the parapets and catwalks, alert to intruders. According to the maps obtained from the BND office, the actual perimeter of land on their side began approximately twenty-five meters ahead. To move any closer would risk detection, and Kaufmann didn't wish to tip off Schleyer. If the German businessman had any idea he was under surveillance, sanctioned or unsanctioned, he would simply close up shop and move his army somewhere else.

The agent handed the binoculars to Jack Grimaldi, who reacted identically to Kaufmann in his surprise. Armored vehicles could be seen doing maneuvers on a far ridge, and troops moved in fire teams, leapfrogging through some kind of live-fire exercise. Grimaldi lowered the night-vision binoculars and shook his head.

"Looks like Mike's got his work cut out for him," Grimaldi observed.

"How many men do you estimate are down there?"

"At least fifty to sixty," Grimaldi replied with a shrug. "Give or take a handful. There's no question about it, though. It's a small army. It also appears they have some top-quality armament." Grimaldi shook his head, adding, "Real state-of-the-art shit down there."

"I thought this was odd, that a man in Edel Schleyer's position should desire so much land. I would not have been quite as suspicious if the permits had been issued for building. Herr Schleyer has enough money to create his own village if he wished."

"And declare himself as absolute ruler, huh?" Grimaldi said.

Kaufmann was not sure how to take his sense of humor, so she just continued with her theory. "The intelligence reports all pointed to Dortmund Linger as the man behind this new army, and I thought him solely responsible for the recent acts of terrorism in my country. I am now believing that Edel Schleyer is responsible for the kidnapping of Dr. Krizova and the deaths of your American agents."

"All the evidence seems to point to this Schleyer guy as the culprit," Grimaldi agreed. "The only question that remains is how to stop him." He hesitated, chewing on his lower lip as he considered the situation. Finally, he turned to face Kaufmann. "Do you think Krizova's being held inside that place?"

"This is possible. We are going to need more information if we are to take action, though. I am not certain how we are to get that information."

"Okay, first things first. We need to find Mike."

"What do you have to report?" Edel Schleyer asked, clutching the telephone receiver to his ear.

"We have captured the American agent," came the static reply. "He refuses to cooperate thus far, but I will get the answers we seek eventually. It is only a matter of time."

"He is no good to us dead, Commander," Schleyer cautioned. "I want him kept alive. I consider him your personal responsibility. There is no benefit in his death if he does not talk first. We *must* know who is behind these sabotage attempts. I can deal better with the enemy when I know who they are.''

"He will not die," Linger said coldly, "and I am quite aware of my responsibilities."

"What about the project?"

"I have acquired new equipment from an alternate supplier, and all is proceeding as planned. Our guest has assured me he will complete the fighter on schedule. The rest of this is child's play. As for Kaufmann, she is becoming a true nuisance. You assured me you would handle her, but she is still alive."

"It is of no consequence," Schleyer retorted. "Gabi will succeed in killing her, now that this meddling American swine is out of the way. With the completion of the jet, the cause will go forward. We will take our war to the Americans, and they will regret the day they ever tried to subjugate the German people."

"I would caution you against overconfidence," Linger stated tightly. "Completion of the project is only part of the goal. We must also make certain we tie up the loose ends."

"I do not need to be lectured, Commander," Schleyer countered. "You have enough to keep you busy there, and all is going as planned here. I have everything under control. Lincoln was very helpful in supplying us with the American agent, and Gabrielle simply tied the noose for us."

"You realize, of course," Linger offered, "that we cannot allow him to live. He is just one of many loose ends."

"I am aware of that. We have to keep him alive for now. I have received reports the Americans sent another agent. He escaped with Kaufmann after a brief firefight at the airport. My sources inform me he was trying to smuggle weapons into the country. He was traveling under the name of Joseph Grimes. They killed two of my men and are currently in hiding. The weapons are with the customs now, so we can assume they will be relatively safe there.''

''What do you plan to do?''

''For now, I will do nothing. Eventually, this man will attempt to make contact with Lincoln. When he does, Lincoln has instructions on what to do. Just like Belasko, this Grimes will have a nasty surprise waiting for him. Until then, we must continue with our plans. Regarding the BND woman, she is simply an annoyance. You should not have allowed her to slip through your fingers. Now she has become a skeleton in your closet. A skeleton you have burdened me with burying.''

''I offered to take her out. It was your preference to handle her personally.''

''Either way, with the fighter almost finished and the American now under control, there is very little she can do. The Iron Skull will succeed, Commander. Mark my words.''

''I am fully confident in your plans.''

''In the meantime, I think I shall come there and speak with the American directly. I am most interested in what he has to say. Prepare for my arrival. I will depart within the hour.''

''It shall be as you wish,'' Linger announced.

Edel Schleyer set the telephone down and shook his head. They had lost nearly one-eighth of their force in capturing the meddling American agent. Schleyer wasn't completely pleased with Gabrielle Reinmaul's performance, but they had suspected the American might resist. This Mike Belasko was definitely resourceful.

Schleyer had a personal interest in the mysterious American. According to Linger, Belasko had taken out most of their men on his own. Such talent could be useful to the Iron Skull. Perhaps he would be a suitable replacement for Dortmund Linger. The former BND commander had become disrespectful and argumentative over the past month. It could have been the stress of their deadline, but Schleyer didn't trust Linger. He believed it was more Linger's personal bid for power.

The men of the Iron Skull might have been loyal to Linger's authority, but they also knew who their true meal ticket was. Linger didn't have a dime to his name, in actuality. Linger's wealth had been amassed by Schleyer. If the commander proved loyal, he would get his money. If not...

Schleyer commanded a guard to notify the driver he would be leaving.

"I DON'T THINK we should try to get closer," Jack Grimaldi protested. "It's risky, and we're hardly equipped to bring that whole pissed-off crew down on our heads."

"I would agree that it is extreme," Kaufmann concurred, "but we must have more information."

Grimaldi shook his head as he peered through the binoculars again. "It's too dangerous. If we—"

His words trailed off as he squinted through the night-vision device. In the hazy green of the magnified field, he could see a limousine pull up and stop in front of the castle entrance. From his vantage point, he could see a man leaving the castle and walking briskly toward the limousine. Grimaldi increased the magnification, bringing the man closer, but he still didn't recognize him. He was tall and good-looking, with an air of authority and a heavy escort of men armed with Uzis.

Grimaldi passed the NVD to Kaufmann. "Focus on the front gate. Do you recognize that man?"

The woman quickly surveyed the same scene as Grimaldi, shaking her head slightly. "Mmm...I am not sure, but that could be Edel Schleyer. It is difficult to tell from here."

"Whoever it is, he's damned important. That's no VW he's riding in, and those aren't toys being toted by that group of guards. We need to follow them."

"He will have to take this road to leave," Kaufmann informed him. "It is the only one in or out of the compound. Let's go!"

As they left their observation site and headed back toward the vehicle, Grimaldi began to ponder the situation. Some guy named Schleyer was amassing a large army. According to Kaufmann, Schleyer was connected with Dortmund Linger, the mercenary Stony Man believed was directly connected with the disappearance of Dr. Vasec Krizova. None of it was making sense to Grimaldi, and he knew they were going to need some answers soon. He also wondered where Mack Bolan was when they needed him most.

11

When Mack Bolan regained consciousness, the first thing he realized was his body temperature was continuing to fall. He wasn't shivering anymore. His feet were completely numb, and his hands raw from the rope. He swung just slightly from whatever was holding him off the ground. He listened carefully several minutes before finally deciding the room was empty. His captors had gone for now, probably leaving a guard outside the door. Linger wouldn't trust Bolan's resourcefulness enough not to leave at least one sentry posted.

Not that there was any chance of escape, although the Executioner always liked to think there was still reason to have hope. He wasn't dead yet, and that had to count for something.

As Bolan hung there, he willed himself to recap the events leading up to his capture. When Brognola approached him about this job, Bolan was skeptical. The disappearance of CIA operatives and a Czech scientist wasn't in his normal realm of operations. Only the high-tech jet fighter and the threat of a new terrorist organization would pique Bolan's interest.

Since the defeat of the Bader-Meinhof Gang in the late 1970s, Germany hadn't been a regular target of terrorist attacks, nor the origin of any new factions. The BND and police were known for their ruthless tactics against terrorism—it was a problem the Federal Republic of Germany took seriously. Antiterrorist tactics were part of the mandatory training just for police recruits, not to mention the regular military and the special-operations groups. Germany was also rumored to have an antiterrorist group so secret, it didn't even have a name.

Shortly after Bolan arrived in Frankfurt, a group of well-armed, well-trained men tried to kill him. They were equipped with weapons, uniforms and luxury sedans. That would indicate good funding, funding that pointed to more money than a mercenary group the size of Linger's would have on hand. The hangar for the plane hadn't been built from scratch. Such a construction project would have cost hundreds of thousands just for materials.

There was also the attack on him and Jütta Kaufmann outside the hotel. That ambush had been well coordinated. Only fate and a bit of luck brought them through that one. Following that, dead CIA agents start to pop up, and some woman connected with the CIA sprung a careless and futile ambush only to lead Bolan into a more elaborate trap.

The Executioner was still kicking himself for that mistake.

With some partial bit of information, the soldier had walked into the trap without the proper equipment or precautions having been taken. Regardless of the fact Bolan intended a soft probe, he jepardized the mission by putting Krizova in the line of fire and allowing himself to be captured so easily. Jütta Kaufmann tried to warn him that Dortmund Linger was a clever and experienced professional. Bolan read the intelligence himself on Linger, and still he'd fallen for what had so obviously been a lure.

But blaming himself for a mistake wasn't helping matters, and it certainly wasn't going to do anything to get him out of there. He needed to concentrate on what all warriors should when taken prisoner. Escape. That was the priority now, and Bolan let the wheels turn as he considered his options.

Getting untied wouldn't be a problem with his hands in front of him, but he would first need to get to the ground. He wondered if he would even be able to stand, let alone walk. He could no longer feel his toes or feet. He needed to stay awake; that was the important part. Bolan licked his lips. They were cracked and stiff. A cold ball was already settling at the pit of his stomach.

He couldn't remember the last time he'd been in such a demoralizing predicament.

Bolan moved his fingers, twisting inside the ropes and grimacing against the rubbing of skin already raw. Several tries and a brief period of tingling finally seemed to restore some circulaton and sense of touch to his hands. A frantic search revealed a cold and pointed metal object between his thumbs. He was hung on a simple hook, probably used for hauling around large sides of beef. That would confirm Bolan's suspicions that he was inside some kind of large meat freezer.

He was considering his next option when the sound of a door opening reached his ears. Bolan turned his head, then decided to play possum. As long as he was still out, Linger and his men would take no pleasure in torturing him further. Bolan's stomach twinged with the reminders of the abuse he had already suffered.

Quiet footfalls drew closer. Suddenly, Bolan felt a warm hand touch his foot, then a spot on the inside of his thigh. Bolan could only surmise the individual was checking for arterial pulse points. That would indicate someone with a good working knowledge of the human body.

An unfamiliar voice whispered, "Mr. Belasko? Mr. Belasko, wake up. Wake up, please."

The sudden whiff of ammonia assaulted his nostrils, and Bolan pulled his head backward reflexively. There was no way out of it now. Whoever stood below knew he was awake. He would have to take his chances. Bolan kept his voice quiet as he replied.

"Who are you?"

"My name is Vasec Krizova."

"Dr. Krizova?"

"That is correct. I am sorry you are in this situation. I realize all of this is my fault. I should have never created that jet. I should have just kept my designs to myself. I should have kept my mouth shut, and nobody would have to suffer for my greed. Those Japanese gentlemen died because I—"

"Look, Dr. Krizova," Bolan rasped, "We don't have time for this. If you're really sorry, you can start showing it by helping me get down from here."

"I will help you, Mr. Belasko, but you must first promise me something."

"I'll get you out of here, don't worry about that."

"No, I do not care for myself. I am speaking of my daughter, Mila. Edel Schleyer is holding her somewhere— I do not know where. They have been using her against me, to coerce me into building this fighter. I have stalled them as long as I can." The man's voice became choked with emotion. "I cannot hold them off any longer, and I am most afraid for Mila's safety. You must promise me that if I help you to escape, you will find Mila and get her away from these terrible people."

"I can't prom—"

"You must!" Krizova countered.

His voice echoed in the confines of the frozen prison, and Bolan tightened up, bracing himself for the sound of the guards to enter. All was quiet for nearly a minute, the only sound audible the gasps and muffled whimpers of a man crying for the life of his only remaining family. Bolan could understand Krizova's fears and pain. The Executioner had seen his own family, and close friends, fall under the devices of some organization thriving on terror for nothing more than profit.

Krizova's voice was quiet again. "You must help her, Mr. Belasko. I care nothing for my own life."

"Yes, but other people do, Dr. Krizova. There is more to this than just your life, or your daughter's. There are the lives of hundreds of thousands of people at stake. At least I know that there is a connection between Schleyer and Linger now."

"Yes," Krizova breathed.

Bolan could feel something warm being wrapped around his feet, and a wool blanket was tossed over his shoulders and wrapped around his front. The blanket was extremely warm, and Bolan shivered as he felt his body temperature immediately begin to rise.

"I have plugged in that electric blanket," Krizova said. "That is a special chemical pack I have wrapped around your feet. I stole them from the infirmary."

"Thanks," Bolan replied. "Now, tell me about the layout of this place. Where are we right now?"

"We are in the cooler, off the kitchen. There is no prison area, so Commander Linger ordered you kept here until it can be decided what to do with you. I overheard him talking with Schleyer. They intend to go forward with their plans. They are going to use the fighter on American soil, destroying a large area, then land troops to mop up."

"With one fighter?" Bolan said disbelievingly. "How do they propose to do that? American defenses could easily repel such a minuscule attack."

"They are not going to attack the mainland. They are going after an alternate target."

"Which is?"

"A military installation on an island somewhere in the Pacific Ocean."

"What island?"

"They did not say this to me personally," Krizova replied. "I am not sure about all of their plans. They have decided to keep you alive for the moment. There is no way I can ever leave here alive, Mr. Belasko. Surely, when I have completed the jet, I will have outlived my usefulness to them. But you can get out of here and find my daughter."

"I would be happy to get both you and your daughter out of Frankfurt alive, Dr. Krizova, but my first objective is to destroy that fighter."

"I promise to take care of that," Krizova whispered hoarsely. "It is my design, and I know its weaknesses. You must find Mila and get her away from Edel Schleyer. Once I know that is done, I will sabotage the plane myself."

Bolan considered his options. He didn't really have any, and it seemed a futile gesture to try to argue with the Czech scientist. Bolan had neither the knowledge nor the means to blow up the fighter externally. Its special hull would protect it from conventional means of destruction, and damage to internal components would only delay the plans of Linger's men.

Bolan finally conceded.

"All right, I give you my word I'll find your daughter."

"I will believe you are a man who keeps your word."

"Linger mentioned something called the Iron Skull," Bolan inquired. "What is that?"

"It is his personal army. A group of mercenaries. There used to be over one hundred, but rumor has it you eliminated approximately twenty percent of their forces. The last count I heard was fifteen dead."

"I counted maybe twenty guns when I first penetrated this place," Bolan interjected. "Where are the rest of them?"

"I do not know. I must assume wherever the rest of the

men are hiding with Schleyer, and that is where Mila is. Right now, there is a small crew working with me. The third shift. Other than the two sentries outside the kitchen, the rest of the force is bedded down for the night. You should be able to get out undetected. I have heard Schleyer is coming here to personally oversee your interrogation. They obviously consider you a very dangerous man, Mr. Belasko.''

"Well, I'm not very dangerous hanging up here. Help get me down."

"I cannot do that."

"What?"

"The only way to get you down would be to lower you on the lift. The guards would surely hear that. After you are warm enough, you should be able to climb the cable and disengage your hands from that hook. You are only about one meter off the floor. I have your weapons and clothes stored in a crate. They will be marked with a red food-inspection label. In the rear of the cooler is a door, which will lead you to the launch tunnel. Bear left, and the tunnel will lead you to an entrance near the Main River."

"Will there be resistance along the way?"

"There are guards at the tunnel entrance, but I do not know how many. Rumors are that it is heavily patrolled, since that is the only route by which vehicles may enter or leave. I must go now. If I am gone too long, I will be missed. If that happens, your chances of escape will be zero. I am sorry about this, Mr. Belasko, but it is the best I can do right now."

"Okay, fine," Bolan acquiesced, "but answer one more question. When is the fighter scheduled to be completed?"

"In two days," Krizova answered quickly. "Goodbye, Mr. Belasko, and good luck."

With that, Krizova departed and Bolan was left alone again. The Executioner waited about fifteen minutes while his body warmed. He was tempted to just stay there. Being warm was enough of a pleasure that he could have just surrendered to the comfort of it all and fallen asleep. There was work to be done, though, and Bolan knew he had to get moving. If Krizova was right, Bolan didn't have much time before Schleyer and Linger launched their plans.

When he could feel himself reach peak efficiency, Bolan wrapped his hands around the chilled cable. His arm muscles were taut with the strain as he hoisted himself up until he was certain his bindings were free of the hook. He dropped to the floor, the soles of his feet slapping the ice-cold tile floor of the meat freezer. Bolan ignored the lightning jolt of pain that shot up his bad ankle.

He crouched and ripped the blindfold from his face. The cooler was bathed in blue-white lights mounted in three corners. Bolan was thankful that his time spent in the darkness hadn't been met with the harsh glare of bright lights. He waited a moment, hunched below the hook in the blanket until he was sure of his bearings.

Bolan rose and padded to the crate. Inside were his blacksuit and weapons, and even the other frag grenade he'd lifted off the watchtower guard. Krizova had been thorough. The soldier used the Ka-bar to sever his bonds. He dressed quickly in the blacksuit, then donned his weaponry. He went back to the hook and collected the blanket, storing it in the empty crate along with the heat packs, then hid the crate behind some large fruit boxes.

The Executioner headed for the rear door, then stopped short as an idea came to him. He palmed the grenade and walked over to the entrance. The freezer door had a push-bar latching system that swung the door inward, with a pull-handle device on the inside to prevent accidental imprisonment inside the cooler. He yanked the pin from the grenade and wedged it between the door handle and the frame.

Whoever opened the door would be in for a nasty surprise.

The Executioner took up the Steyr in a ready position and exited through the rear door as Krizova had indicated. He ascended the sloping, narrow corridor, thankful for the relative warmth of the underground complex. The corridor ended at the launch tunnel, and he peered around the corner to his right.

The launch tunnel sloped downward to the hangar, roughly two hundred yards from Bolan's position. Steel wall supports welded to overhead girders stabilized the tunnel which had been cut from sheer rock and limestone. The tunnel was well lit but deserted. Bolan checked both directions before entering into the tunnel, alert for any opposition.

He turned to his left and began his long climb toward freedom.

As THEY ENTERED the city limits of Frankfurt, Jack Grimaldi turned an amazed expression on Jütta Kaufmann.

"I still can't believe you drove that whole road without lights."

"I was raised in that part of the country," she replied graciously. "I know the road well, so it was nothing to follow them undetected."

"Well, I'm still impressed," Grimaldi said. "Where do you think this guy is leading us? To Krizova maybe?"

"I do not know," she said with a shrug.

Kaufmann concentrated on staying several car lengths behind the limousine that carried Edel Schleyer and a score of armed bodyguards as they crossed one of the several bridges leading from the southern part of the city to the northern part. They weren't equipped to handle a firefight against a group of trained soldiers, and Kaufmann felt the best method of observation at present was stealth.

Jack Grimaldi wasn't about to argue with her. "How about a guess?"

"I am hoping they will lead me to Dortmund Linger. If that is so, I will follow the orders of my superiors and eliminate the commander. He is a dangerous man, and I have sought him for many years."

"Do you honestly think that killing Linger is going to change anything?" Grimaldi demanded. "I mean, really…this other guy could just go on with whatever they have planned, and it wouldn't make any difference."

"I do not believe that killing Commander Linger will stop Schleyer, Herr Grimes. However, Linger has been responsible for many terrorist actions in my country, and the security of Germany is at risk as long as he is alive."

"I can understand that," Grimaldi replied easily. "But the security of the United States is also at risk. Now, I appreciate you saving my ass back there at the airport, but that doesn't mean I'll compromise my mission."

"I thought you wanted to find your friend."

"Belasko can take care of himself," Grimaldi countered. "Don't worry about that. What we need to do right now is find out what this Schleyer guy you keep talking about is up to, and how he connects with Linger."

"Precisely," Kaufmann replied triumphantly.

The limousine suddenly turned left at the far side of the bridge, barely fitting its wide frame down the narrow gravel road leading toward the bank of the Main River. The German agent swung her vehicle in a U turn halfway across the bridge to the honking horns of angry motorists and went back to the turnoff. She passed the gravel road and swung the car to the shoulder just short of the bridge entrance.

"Follow me," she ordered.

They bailed from the car and hoofed it down the trail, jogging to make up for lost time. Kaufmann suddenly plunged into the woods on the left, and Grimaldi had no choice but to follow. Branches whipped at his face and left furrows in the material of his flight uniform as the woman led him through the thickets. Abruptly, the pair emerged on the shore of the river in time to see the limousine on the road overhead.

The car looked as if it were going to drive right into the woods, but in the light of the moon the brush suddenly gave way to a well-lit entrance. The sound of hydraulics could be heard as the forest floor literally opened upward. Kaufmann and Grimaldi watched in stunned amazement as the limousine seemed to disappear from view. They looked at each other a moment before scrambling up the hill to where the limousine had entered, barely fitting through the entrance before the ground seemed to collapse down upon them. The metal door, camouflaged by forestry on its exterior, sealed them inside with the unquestionable finality of clanging locks.

The tunnel sloped downward, reinforced walls of concrete and rock lighted by bright lamps. Grimaldi and Kaufmann could see the limousine stop at a checkpoint of armed guards ahead. One of the rear doors opened, and a gunman got out, followed by five other armed guards. The first man out of the limo conversed in hushed tones with the apparent leader of the four armed guards at the entrance. The man then returned to the limo, leaving the other guards with the group at the checkpoint, and the vehicle continued down the tunnel.

"Where the hell are we at?" Grimaldi whispered.

They were observing the action from the shadows of large, boulderlike formations at the entrance to the tunnel. Kaufmann appeared as impressed by the vast tunnel as Grimaldi, her eyes wide as she studied the contours of their new find. The idea of such an underground complex within the bowels of Frankfurt was nearly unfathomable. To keep this place a secret had to have cost Schleyer a fortune. It wasn't any wonder now why she'd been unable to find Linger.

"I am not sure," she whispered back. "We are in some kind of underground complex."

"Well, I can see that," Grimaldi shot back. "But why are they going to all this trouble and expense?"

"I must believe that they are hiding something down there." She nodded toward the tunnel.

"Something like a jet fighter?" Grimaldi proposed with raised eyebrows.

The horror of his statement weighed as heavy as the steel door now trapping them inside the compound. If Schleyer and Linger had somehow found a way to make Krizova construct the jet, there was more at stake than just a few lives taken by Linger. The gravity of the situation had suddenly become apparent. Grimaldi had suspected the possibility early on. Stony Man had been clear; if the fighter was being built, and Grimaldi couldn't steal it, then he was supposed to destroy it.

The ace pilot was concerned about finding Bolan, as well. Although he'd told Kaufmann that Bolan could take care of himself, he didn't feel quite as confident. They should have heard something by now. Striker was either dead, captured or awaiting the right moment to act. With any luck, he was already gearing for action, and the German agent and Grimaldi could find some way to assist him. The first step would be to escape and find him.

"Mike needs to know about this place," Grimaldi hissed.

"You do not think he must already know?"

"I can't make that assumption. What we need to do now is get the hell out of here, before—"

Screeching alarms suddenly wailed through the tunnel, and the lights flickered with each burst of the buzzing alert. Grimaldi and Kaufmann looked wildly in all directions, then noticed six of the nine guards turning to stare in their direction. The guards swung their weapons around, training them on Grimaldi and Kaufmann.

"Oh, shit!" Grimaldi spit. "I think we're in trouble!"

The pair drew their weapons, ducking behind the makeshift cover as their enemy approached. The muzzles of the gunmen's weapons flashed, the sounds of autofire mind numbing as they fired their first volleys. They obviously weren't looking to take prisoners.

As the 9 mm rounds zinged overhead, chipping out stone and ricocheting off the metal of the entrance door, Grimaldi considered their options. They couldn't allow themselves to be captured. Surely this group would eventually extract enough information to jeopardize the mission—particularly when it came to Mack Bolan. They were clearly outgunned, but it didn't really matter. Grimaldi figured that if he was going to die right there, it made sense to take as many with him as he could.

"Are you ready to kick ass?" he yelled at Kaufmann, jacking the slide on his P-7 and chambering a round.

"You are in charge," she replied with a smile.

"Since when?" Grimaldi asked.

"Since I decided I will not have to take responsibility for your death. Instead, you must be responsible for mine."

"Oh," Grimaldi said, popping up over the rock to sight in on his first target. "Well, it was a pleasure knowing you."

12

Bolan heard the gunfire ahead and dropped flat to the ground.

He could barely discern the outline of a large vehicle coming straight toward him, as sirens resounded throughout the tunnel. He checked his rear flank, then examined the walls on either side. There was nowhere to hide. He would have to take the oncoming vehicle. As it drew nearer, he saw it was a limousine. An initial inspection didn't indicate it was armored. Nonetheless, Bolan wished he hadn't left the frag grenades in the freezer.

The soldier stayed flat until the limousine rolled within fifty yards. The driver obviously hadn't spotted him. Bolan counted to three, then rose and aimed his Steyr at the windshield. He squeezed the trigger, rushing the vehicle in a flat sprint. The windshield gave way, and the bullets found their mark, drilling holes through the driver's face. The limo careened to the left, smashing against the girders and grinding to a halt.

A gunman immediately exited the rear of the vehicle, and Bolan triggered his Mpi69 again. The 9 mm Parabellum rounds ripped through the man's body, slamming him backward into the vehicle's interior. The soldier reached the open door and peered into the darkened back seat. A tall, lean man with distinguished features stared back at him. The fear was evident in his eyes, although his demeanor seemed calm and collected.

"Out!" Bolan ordered, waving the Steyr.

The older man climbed from the vehicle, and Bolan shoved him to the ground. He didn't recognize the man, and he didn't care who he was at the moment. Escape was still his primary goal as Bolan slid behind the wheel of the limousine. It took several jerky motions to swing the big vehicle around. He aimed the nose of the limo up the slope and tromped the accelerator. Rubber burned on the smooth flooring as the limo accelerated toward the checkpoint.

Bolan ducked behind the wheel as three armed guards ahead fired on him. Their rounds peppered the grille, turning the headlights, hood and radiator into scrap metal. Steam poured from the damaged front as Bolan continued on his escape run. He kept the pedal to the floor, swinging the Steyr in front of him. Aiming the weapon through a broken gap in the windshield, he triggered the weapon. Two of the gunmen dived away from the roaring limo, but the third didn't make it in time. Bolan smashed the merc against the wall, crushing him.

The soldier went EVA on the passenger's side, Steyr at the ready. One Uzi gunner was already on his feet, leveling his weapon for a kill shot, but Bolan beat him to the punch. A hail of 9 mm fire blew out stomach, lungs and heart, the impact twisting the gunner as he discharged his own useless volley of shots. Bolan turned and fired again before the man's partner could regain his feet.

The Executioner spotted a dozen gunmen in the far distance down the tunnel, but a flash in his periphery demanded his more immediate attention. He turned and spotted the Uzi belonging to one of the gunners lying near the tire of the limo. Bolan picked it up and rushed for the cover of a large wall support. The six remaining gunmen had their backs to him, concentrating on something ahead. He couldn't make out who they were firing at.

He used their diverted attention to his advantage.

The soldier stepped from cover and fired both weapons, the Steyr's magazine emptying first. Three of his six targets fell under the fresh assault. He dropped and rolled as the remaining trio whirled to face the new threat. In a brief silence that followed, Bolan heard the distant sounds of repeated pistol shots. Another man went down, arching backward as the pistol shots entered his spine. Whoever was on the far side was creating a cross fire. Bolan didn't wait to identify his allies. He took careful aim and triggered his Uzi. The last pair was punched to the ground, one gunman taking bullets in the abdomen, the other losing his head in the deal.

Bolan didn't rise at first, hesitant to expose himself prematurely.

A head popped up over a far boulder, and Bolan thought he was seeing things. Jack Grimaldi's face broke into a grin, followed by a second form bursting from cover. Jütta Kaufmann ran toward him as Bolan gained his feet.

"Stay there!" he ordered, turning his attention back to the distant figures. "We're about to have company!"

Kaufmann stopped suddenly and turned to look at Grimaldi helplessly.

"Sarge!" Grimaldi called. "There should be a switch somewhere there. A release for a trapdoor."

Bolan threw him a gesture of understanding, then began to search the walls. He was about to give up when he spotted two levers. One was larger than the other, capped with a bright red sphere, the smaller one with a yellow one. He hesitated, finally yanking the smaller lever. He turned to the sound of grinding gears and the hiss of hydraulics as the wall behind Grimaldi seemed to melt away.

"Move!" Bolan yelled.

Kaufmann turned and headed back in the direction of the doors as Grimaldi waved for them to hurry. Bolan timed the opening of the hatchway, the numbers ticking in his head. It was about a forty-yard run uphill, and he would have to make that distance in under ten seconds. He spun to see the armed gunman now running toward him, making poor time in their uphill trek.

Bolan sprayed autofire in their direction. That would keep heads down. He turned back to see Kaufmann and Grimaldi in the clearing beyond the doors. The soldier counted to three, then threw the lever and raced up the hill, his legs pumping, heart thudding in his ears, as he pushed against the smooth and slippery flooring of the access tunnel. He drew closer.

Twenty yards…fifteen…ten…

He dropped and rolled at the last second, feeling the metal brush the back of his shoulders as he dived through the narrowing gap. Grimaldi rushed forward, helping Bolan to his feet and slapping his shoulders with marked enthusiasm.

"Am I glad to see you!" Grimaldi exclaimed.

"Same here," Bolan replied, cracking into a smile.

He turned toward Kaufmann who rushed forward and threw her arms his neck. Bolan let the moment pass, then pushed her away gently.

"Let's get the hell out of here. You got wheels nearby?"

"Roger that," Grimaldi replied.

As they trotted toward the spot where Kaufmann had parked, Bolan looked at Grimaldi. "What are you doing here?"

"Well, the chief figured you might need a little help," Grimaldi cracked. He jerked a thumb in Kaufmann's direction. "We didn't know you already had someone beautiful and competent on your side."

"I take it this wasn't your idea, then?"

Grimaldi smiled. "Are you kidding? I was sunning myself in Bermuda when they called me."

"Yeah, right."

DORTMUND LINGER ASSISTED Schleyer to his feet as the dust settled around them, and the expression on the man's face told Linger his master wasn't happy with the turn of events. The merc leader wasn't nearly as concerned with Schleyer's anger as he was with the escape of their prisoner. Somehow, the man had escaped from the cooler, retrieved his clothing and weapons and turned the tables on them. The whole fiasco left Linger with egg on his face and cost him another dozen of his men. Now the enemy was free and knew the location of both Krizova and the fighter. This wasn't good at all.

"I trust you have an explanation for this?" Schleyer asked coolly, incensed as he waved at the death and destruction around them.

"He escaped," Linger replied matter-of-factly.

"I can see that, Commander," Schleyer replied. "I would like to know how he escaped while he was in your custody."

"Someone from the inside must have helped him."

That caused Schleyer to pause and think a moment. "Krizova?"

"Possibly, although I am not sure how. The shift was thin. It could have been anybody."

"Was there any damage to the plane?"

"None. But Belasko now knows where to find us and what our plans are. With this information, he could create a real problem for us. We must launch our assault immediately, before he can stop us."

"The fighter is not ready."

"Then we will have to launch the assault without it," Linger protested. "My men are ready. We have been training for this operation more than a year, and the jet will not give us that much of an advantage. We must attack by some other means. Perhaps submarine, or even hijack a commercial jet liner."

"No!" Schleyer shouted. "We will do no such thing. We must find Belasko and eliminate him."

"You said it yourself," Linger argued, waving in the direction of the guards who had set about cleaning up and establishing a security perimeter. "We cannot spare any more men. We are already short of our full complement, and there is no time to recruit more."

"We must stop thinking in such abstract terms," Schleyer proposed. "We must develop a plan of action, something that will end with favorable results."

"We have tried everything," Linger snapped. "Direct assault, silent ambush, entrapment. Belasko is not alone. Kaufmann is helping him, as well as that other American, Grimes. They are presently in hiding, and we have no way of finding them. A few well-placed charges could destroy the launch tunnel, and set your precious timetable back another month. We have no alternative but to launch the attack immediately."

"We do have one more trick up our sleeve," Schleyer finally replied.

"What's that?"

"Contact Herr Lincoln, and tell him to come here."

"What do you have in mind?"

Schleyer appeared thoughtful before replying. "Belasko was foolish enough to launch an assault on us without planning. You of all people should know that a professional soldier would not make the same mistake twice."

"I don't follow," Linger replied.

"Remember that my contacts said Herr Grimes attempted to smuggle a crate of weapons and demolitions into the country, but customs impounded the material."

"I understand now. You think he will try to obtain this equipment before attempting a sabotage effort."

"Exactly," Schleyer replied. "And when he does, my

friends will be waiting for him. This time, there will be no escape.''

Edel Schleyer's laughter echoed along the length of the launch tunnel.

JÜTTA KAUFMANN DROPPED Bolan and Grimaldi at the hotel, then headed to a nearby market to buy food. In her absence, Bolan explained what had transpired since his arrival in Frankfurt. Grimaldi listened with interest, then fell silent for a time as he considered what Bolan had told him. Finally, the ace pilot lit a cigarette and produced the attaché case filled with the information from Stony Man.

He showed Bolan the picture of Linger and Niktor Hess.

Bolan tapped the photo of Hess. "I took this guy out early on.''

"It's no small wonder that Linger wants your blood, then,'' Grimaldi announced through a cloud of smoke. "That's Niktor Hess. He used to be Linger's right-hand man.''

"Tough.''

"That's only the half of it. The man inside the limousine that you left behind?''

"Schleyer?''

"Yep.'' Grimaldi said, nodding. "In the flesh. We saw him get into that limo at some fortress he's got, about an hour's drive south of here.''

"So you followed him, and that's how you ended up at their secret complex.''

"There's more to it than that. When we were there, we witnessed probably fifty to sixty soldiers. It was nothing shy of a small army, Sarge. They had both small arms and heavy firepower. They were doing some kind of night maneuvers that included some pretty heavy stuff. I saw Hummers, track APCs with mounted machine guns and mortars. There were even a couple of light tanks, and a shitload of assault vehicles. You know, the kind we've seen them use for beachfronts. They were real similar to those sea-to-land crafts used by our Special Forces.''

"That makes sense," Bolan replied with a short nod. "Krizova told me the jet fighter was only being used to clear a path. Apparently, Schleyer's financing the Iron Skull, his team, to assault an American-controlled territory in the Pacific."

"My God," Grimaldi said. "What the hell could they be up to?"

"My guess is one of the Hawaiian Islands. Possibly Oahu. If they could take possession of Diamond Head, the military base there would be worth a lot. The limited troop strength is just one of the advantages, as well as its isolation from American forces on the mainland."

"That's insane, Sarge. There must be more to it than that."

"From everything I know about Schleyer, he's anything but sane, Jack," Bolan countered. "The only thing I can't figure out is where the fighter fits into all of this. I have an idea of its capabilities. But why go to such an elaborate plan to kidnap Krizova, build the jet and spend millions of dollars just for this? If they have a specific objective, I could think of easier ways to accomplish it."

"I think I can answer that. The President released technical information on the fighter to Hal."

"Well," Bolan growled, "better late than never."

"This plane is said to be nearly twice as fast as any fighter in existence. It's virtually undetectable by radar, and it comes with one hell of a devastating weapons complement. Hal thought we might be able to salvage the mission if I could just get my hands on it."

"What do you mean?"

"He wants us to try and steal the damned thing. Can you believe it?"

"No, that's not what I mean. I'm more concerned with this salvage you're talking about."

"Well, when we didn't hear from you—"

"I knew there was something about Dan Lincoln I didn't like. He must be on someone's payroll. I'd be willing to bet he was the one who leaked the meet to Linger, and directly responsible for the death of Carter Wiley."

"Let me guess," Grimaldi interjected. "He claims he contacted us, right?"

"Not only that," Bolan continued, "but he also set up the meet between me and this woman, someone named Gabi."

"Gabi?" Kaufmann asked from behind them.

Both men whirled to the sound of her voice. She had entered the room so quietly, neither one of them had even heard it.

"What did this woman look like?"

Bolan described her, and Kaufmann nodded with an expression of recognition.

"That sounds like Gabrielle Reinmaul. She's a known associate of Edel Schleyer, and a former agent with the BND. We have suspected her of coercion with Dortmund Linger for some time now."

"The plot thickens," Grimaldi quipped.

"I'm not concerned about her right now," Bolan stated. "We need to focus on this fortress you two saw. You estimate about sixty guns, Jack?"

Grimaldi nodded. "Give or take."

"I need to see this place. With that much equipment, we can really make a large dent in the operation by taking out the fortress. No landing force, no operation. Simple."

"Okay, you're the boss," Grimaldi replied. "But what about that hangar and the plane?"

"Krizova promised me he would take care of sabotaging the plane. He's the only one that knows that fighter well enough, so it stands to reason he should be able to destroy it.''

"You understand that Linger and Schleyer will kill him when they find out he destroyed their plans?''

"It can't be helped. Krizova has a daughter he believes is being held captive by Schleyer. He seemed to think that if we found the main force of the Iron Skull, we would also find Mila. I gave him my word I would rescue her if he helped me to escape. I intend to keep that promise. It only makes it convenient that I can take out their private army at the same time.''

"That's going to be tough," Grimaldi said. "Where are we going to get the firepower for this little operation? Mission control sent a whole crate full of your favorite toys on the flight with me, along with enough demolitions to probably level a city block. The problem is, they're sitting in the customs warehouse near the Frankfurt airport.''

Bolan turned in his chair to face Kaufmann who was preparing a meal of currywurst, boiled potatoes and bread and cheese. She smiled knowingly, winking at him as she cut up the onions and dumped them into the pan. The scent of frying sausage wafted into the main room of the hotel, and both men suddenly realized how hungry they were.

"Jütta, is there any way we can get those weapons out of customs?''

"I believe I can help with this. Smuggling illegal contraband into Germany is a matter for the BND. It would only take an order from my superiors, and we could impound the weapons.''

She brought the bread and cheese out on a tray, along with a fresh carafe of coffee. She set them down on the table, then turned to face Bolan, propping her hands on her hips.

"I could tell the commissioner that I caught Herr Grimes trying to smuggle them in, and that he was killed in the shootout at the airport. My superiors would not know the difference. If I tell him the weapons were for Mike Belasko, he would cooperate in a moment."

"I only see one problem with that plan," Grimaldi said.

"What's that?" Belasko asked.

Grimaldi turned his attention to the German agent. "Didn't you say those two guys we killed were carrying forged identification?"

"*Ja,* that is true."

"That means that they might expect some type of retrieval operation. If there is a leak in the CIA, and this contact *is* dirty, they're probably going to be waiting for us. The whole thing could go real sour in a minute."

"I've already considered that possibility," Bolan said. "In fact, I'm counting on it."

13

Dan Lincoln was jolted awake by the ringing of his telephone. His drive to Prague had left him exhausted. He rolled over and looked at the clock. Whoever the hell was calling at four o'clock in the morning had better have a good reason for waking him out of a sound sleep. Lincoln fumbled for the phone, pressing it to his ear as he smacked at the pastiness of his morning mouth.

"Yeah?"

"Herr Lincoln?" It was Dortmund Linger.

Lincoln sat up in bed, immediately awake at the sound of the mercenary's voice. Edel Schleyer wasn't the most forgiving man, and Lincoln suspected the hit against Belasko had failed. Linger wouldn't have any other reason for calling him so early in the morning. Something was wrong.

"What is it?"

"Our mutual friend would like you to come to the complex. He wishes to speak with you regarding the American agent."

"Did he get away?"

"Just come to the compound," Linger ordered. "Then we will discuss this at length."

"Give me thirty minutes," Lincoln replied. He slammed down the phone.

As Lincoln got out of bed and began to dress, he considered the situation. If Gabrielle Reinmaul had failed in her attempt to ambush Belasko, that certainly wasn't his fault. Lincoln had never trusted Edel Schleyer, but he trusted Linger even less. That big dude wasn't playing with a full deck.

The CIA case chief looked around his huge master bedroom. Had the money really been worth it? After all, once you sold out to a man like Schleyer, there was no turning back. Beth Lincoln questioned her husband about their lifestyle. She'd never asked questions about his work in the past, but she wasn't stupid either. Beth knew the CIA didn't pay that well, even for a case chief. Lincoln had told her to mind her own business, and be happy with all they had.

Beth left him, returning to her parents' small home on Cape Cod.

Lincoln chalked up his short marriage to experience. If she couldn't take it, that was no skin off his nose. Yes, it had been worth the money. Lincoln lived like a king. The CIA didn't keep close tabs on him, and his immediate supervisor was stationed in Berlin—that kept him far enough away not to be noticed. Only the recent deaths of two of his agents were attracting attention. Attention that Schleyer and Linger had started with their damned ideals about a new Germany, a Fourth Reich or whatever the hell the Iron Skull was supposed to stand for.

Lincoln figured he had signed up with the devil himself, and there was no turning back now. Schleyer owned Dan Lincoln, which was fine as long as the checks kept rolling in every month. Three hundred grand a year to look the other way and fudge a few case files or reports was no paltry sum. Furthermore, Dan Lincoln wasn't any cheapskate. He'd known men in his position who would have sold out their own mothers for one-quarter of what he was making.

That didn't make him a cheat. That made him smart.

As Lincoln headed for his car, he couldn't contain his curiosity regarding Belasko. In their two meetings, Lincoln had found something cold and arrogant about the man. Probably just another G-man, working for pennies while he suffered at the hands of American politicians, politicians who gave no thought for those on the front lines. Men like Lincoln worked themselves ragged, trying to maintain a hopeless peace and rearranging whole governments in secret so that those same clowns could shine in the public eye.

The most disgusting thing was those same political entities would then turn on the men who made them great— just as a pack turned on an alpha male too old and weak to lead any longer. Somewhere along the line, if Lincoln could turn a profit from such backbiting, he would do so. He had no use for his government and no loyalty to the flag. He'd been betrayed too many times.

Although he was only thirty-two, Lincoln knew his life was winding down. If he'd been smart, he would have saved the money Schleyer paid him in a special account, and split the country when things were too hot. The nest egg wasn't quite large enough. Sure, he had enough to live on. A small fortune to most Third World countries, where he could live like a king until the day of his death.

That wasn't the problem.

The problem was his government. If he disappeared, the company would surely send someone after him, and it cost a lot of money to buy silence. If Lincoln was going to disappear off the face of the earth, he was going to have to find some way to acquire the money to do it. He'd become quite accustomed to his life-style, and it would take more money than he had stashed.

Maybe the meeting with Schleyer wasn't such a bad idea. He could ask for a little more cash. Another hundred and a quarter would do it. Lincoln could cover his tracks real well with that kind of bread, and nobody would ever be the wiser. Yeah, he would just disappear from view, and nobody would give a tinker's damn that Daniel Roosevelt Lincoln had ever existed.

As far as Mike Belasko went, that dude was just a minor roadblock to Lincoln's success. Schleyer and Linger would deal with him, if they hadn't already. It was time for Dan Lincoln to be moving on to bigger and better things. He could buy himself a nice place on some tropical island, fill it with wine, women and song, and nobody would ever be able to touch him again. Let them convert some other poor schnook. Maybe Belasko? Perhaps that's why they needed him. Yeah, maybe they wanted him to have a little heart-to-heart with Belasko. A lot of people had jumped onto the bandwagon in the past, and only Carter Wiley had turned his head. Look where it had gotten Wiley. Nice guys did finish last after all.

As he drove to the underground complex, Dan Lincoln daydreamed of palm trees.

SCHLEYER STUDIED Vasec Krizova suspiciously. Nothing in the man's eyes revealed betrayal or treachery. Several of Linger's trusted workers said he had been present for most of the time, only taking one brief break. Krizova had never been seen near the entrance of the launch tunnel, and there was no feasible way he'd been gone long enough to free Bolan. Somehow, the man had escaped on his own. The only other plausible explanation was a traitor in the ranks. If that was the case, this traitor would eventually reveal himself.

The most disturbing factor was that the fighter couldn't be made ready any sooner. That meant Schleyer's Chinese friends would have to take out Belasko successfully. There could be no mistakes, no second chances. They had one try to defeat him, and one try only. After that, the whole operation would be a free-for-all. Schleyer couldn't abide incompetence. Linger had proved himself less than adequate in the past seventy-two hours.

Since Belasko's arrival in Frankfurt, the Iron Skull had experienced nothing but disorganization, chaos and disaster. It was no small miracle the fighter hadn't been damaged somehow in the one-man assault. *One man!* Every time Schleyer thought of it, his blood ran cold. He was surrounded by mercenaries and trained soldiers who couldn't take one man. Was any single soldier truly that good? Belasko was outnumbered, outgunned and outwitted.

Edel Schleyer owned most of Germany. He considered the country his helpless child, one that required ceaseless nurturing and protection. This Belasko had interfered with Schleyer's care of his countrymen, and Schleyer meant to avenge himself on Bolan.

He would deal with the interference once and for all.

"What you are telling me then, *Doktor,* is that you have no idea how this man escaped?"

"I do not," Krizova answered simply.

"You were here with the fighter the whole time?"

"I was here with the exception of one break. We have been over this twice already."

Schleyer slapped the steel-framed table with his fist. "We will go over it a third time, then! We will go over it as many times as I think prudent until I am satisfied you have not lied to me, nor assisted this man's escape! Otherwise, I will personally execute your daughter in front of your eyes!"

"Death would be a welcome relief to slaving away for the greater glory of your imagined empire, Herr Schleyer," Krizova said quietly, looking down at his hands resting in his lap.

"Be careful what you say, Krizova," Linger chimed in. He stood behind Schleyer, looming over his master like a dark shadow. "We have decided you can still work without your tongue, remember?"

"I do not know how this man escaped," Krizova replied, "and you are wasting precious time that would be better spent finishing the fighter."

Schleyer looked up at Linger, who indicated he had no other questions, then the German businessman ordered the guards to escort Krizova back to the hangar. When they were gone, Schleyer rose from his chair and paced around the sparse room adjoining one of the corridors connected to the hangar. He couldn't be sure Krizova wasn't involved in Belasko's escape, but he didn't have proof, either. To kill Mila Krizova would only result in her father's immediate rebellion. It would create a delay they couldn't afford. They *had* to get the fighter working before Bolan tried to return and sabotage their plans.

Schleyer stopped pacing and looked at Linger. "What do you think, Commander?"

"I think he is lying," Linger retorted. "I think he helped Belasko. In fact, I think he was instrumental in the escape. The American had his clothing, his weapons and he knew where to get out. None of my men would have assisted in such treachery. They know I would kill them without question."

"The problem is that he never should have escaped to begin with, Commander Linger," Schleyer reprimanded.

"Forgive me, but this is a construction facility, not a prison. It would be better to keep prisoners at the fortress."

"True," Schleyer said, considering Linger's words. "Okay, when they capture Belasko, I will have him taken directly to the castle. Perhaps he will be able to console Mila Krizova."

There was a brief knock at the door before a man stepped through and saluted Linger.

"Report?"

"Herr Lincoln is present, sir," the soldier replied.

"Send him in."

Dan Lincoln entered, nodding to Linger and Schleyer in turn. Schleyer studied Lincoln with mild interest. The CIA operative had done well for their operations, but Linger was correct in pointing out that his usefulness was coming to an end. There couldn't be any witnesses to their plans, and Schleyer would order Linger to eliminate the CIA man—after they had confirmed Belasko either captured or dead.

Schleyer offered Lincoln a seat. "Make yourself comfortable, Herr Lincoln. May we offer you something to drink?"

"Too early in the morning," Lincoln replied, waving his hand. "What's this all about? I thought you didn't wish to conduct business in person, Mr. Schleyer."

"Normally I would not, Herr Lincoln. However, this is a special situation. This Belasko is causing us all kinds of grief. Plans to apprehend him have failed."

"We need you to help us solve our problem," Dortmund Linger added.

"I have a plan," Schleyer added. "A plan in which you play a vital role."

"Uh-uh, boss, not me," Lincoln said. "Your people were supposed to take care of this guy and you didn't. I did what you asked me to do." He gestured toward Schleyer. "You miss, and now you want me to put my neck on the line? Forget that! I'm not going to have a part in trying to take him out."

"Herr Lincoln," Schleyer replied quietly, "let me remind you of who works for whom. I have paid you well, and neither Commander Linger nor myself tolerate insubordinate behavior. You will do what you are told to do. If not, you shall not live to see another day. Do you understand me?"

Schleyer's tone had the same effect on Lincoln as if

someone had forced him to listen to fingernails being run over a chalkboard. Chills went down his spine, and it seemed as if the temperature in the room had dropped twenty degrees. Lincoln turned to see nothing but cold steel in Linger's expression. The man would murder him without a second thought, and Lincoln knew he had no choice but to cooperate.

"Okay, I'll help you out. But I want some extra thrown in for my trouble, you see? I've got debts to pay. As soon as this job is done, I'm out of here. You got me? I'm splitting, and anything beyond Belasko is just going to have to be someone else's problem."

Schleyer's smile was cold in the dim lights of the room. "That will be fine. Extra money should not be a problem. I give you my personal guarantee that this is the last thing you will ever have to do for the cause."

"Fine," Lincoln replied. "What do you want me to do?"

THE DAWN SUN BROKE through the cloudy horizon. Bolan watched Jütta Kaufmann through the binoculars as she parked her car in front of the customs office. He lay prone on the roof of a private hangar closed for the winter months. The Executioner was counting on his plan to work. It hadn't been difficult for Kaufmann to get the impound order from her supervisor, especially when she told Gerhard the weaponry had been sent to aid Belasko.

Now it was just a matter of waiting to see if Edel Schleyer was as predictable as Bolan suspected. Jack Grimaldi's theory had merit. Schleyer's people had to know the smuggled weapons were intended for use against the Iron Skull. Moreover, if Kaufmann was correct in her belief that Linger still had sympathizers inside the BND, then time was running out. It was fortunate Stony Man had been on its toes when no word was received of how his operation was proceeding—no thanks to the traitorous Dan Lincoln. Bolan would deal with the CIA case chief all in good time.

The first objective had to be fresh firepower.

Kaufmann exited her vehicle and casually waved her credentials at the officer stationed inside the front entrance. Bolan swept the binoculars along the building perimeter. The first target presented itself. A sentry was seated behind a parked panel truck near the far edge of the building, smoking a cigarette. Bolan adjusted the focus. The man looked Asian, possibly Chinese. Something didn't fit there. Maybe Schleyer had turned to outside help.

Bolan lowered the binoculars and brought the shortwave radio close to his lips. The radios had been provided courtesy of Kaufmann's BND connections. They were portable devices, operating on alternating frequencies and equipped with private-line crystals as a failsafe against monitoring. Such tactical features would be an advantage for them.

"Striker to Eagle, do you read?"

"This is Eagle, over." Jack Grimaldi's voice crackled over the line.

"I make a single inside that panel, about two o'clock. Appears to be a lookout. Probably hostile, over?"

"Copy, Striker, I see him, too."

"Might be more unfriendlies in that panel, Eagle. Let's be prepared to take out the trash."

"Roger, the Eagle is in position."

"Copy that. Striker out here."

Bolan ended the transmission and turned his attention back to the truck. Seeing Kaufmann alone would probably make the observer suspicious. The Executioner hoped it didn't backfire on them. He had learned long ago that anything could happen during even the most carefully planned operation. He wasn't infallible and had never claimed to be. Schleyer's orders might simply have been to eliminate anyone showing up to claim the weapons yet open murder of a BND agent didn't seem to be Schleyer's style. It would make more sense to take Kaufmann alive, and make her reveal the location of Grimaldi and Bolan.

Timing would be everything.

KAUFMANN APPROACHED the property officer sitting behind a steel cage and handed him her credentials for inspection. The man looked quickly at the ID, then she produced the order signed by Baldric Gerhard.

"There is a crate which was impounded late last night," she explained. "The pilot was an American who attempted to smuggle weapons into the country. It was believed this individual was planning to use the weapons in a terrorist operation. As a matter of national security, the BND has been ordered to transfer these items to a secured location until final disposition."

"Your paperwork appears to be in order," the officer replied with a nod. "If you would come with me...?"

The property officer buzzed her through a bulletproof door adjoining the cage, and led her through a small corridor into the warehouse proper. The officer verified the number on the crate matched the order, returned the carbon and quickly wrote a receipt ticket for her to sign.

"If you will bring your vehicle to the back, I can have the custodian load it on."

Kaufmann smiled sweetly and winked. "Thank you."

As she went back through the front office, she keyed the radio mike concealed under the left sleeve of her blouse. "*Prost,*" she whispered.

BOLAN WAS ON HIS FEET and crossing the roof to the rear of the hangar bay upon hearing Kaufmann give the German code word. He reached the edge of the roof and vaulted over the side without hesitation. He landed gracefully and shoulder rolled to break his fall. Within moments, he was on his feet and sprinting for the panel van as Kaufmann passed through the vestibule.

Jack Grimaldi was right on schedule. He sidled casually past her, palming the receipt ticket she slipped him as she exited the building. He continued parallel along the front of the customs office and rounded the corner as the woman headed for her car.

Bolan was close enough to see the man in the panel truck moving toward Kaufmann. He fisted the 93-R, selected 3-round bursts and aimed on the run. The trio of 9 mm slugs burned past the man, missing him by a few inches. The Asian had been concentrating so hard on Kaufmann, he hadn't noticed his new opposition. Bolan fired a second burst, again coming close but purposefully missing the target. The Asian grabbed the woman from behind, a Mauser pistol materializing in his hand. He pressed the muzzle against the forehead of his human shield.

The soldier gave the impression of hesitancy as the Asian dragged his hostage back in the direction of the panel truck. Bolan was within forty yards of the truck when five men bailed from the back of it, their machine pistols leaving no doubt about their intentions.

The Executioner lunged behind a stone barricade to his left as the newcomers opened up in unison. He pressed his frame tightly against the barricade as a barrage of lead pelted the back side of six-inch-thick concrete. Sharp fragments of stone rained on him. The soldier holstered his Beretta, trading it for the Desert Eagle. He waited for a lull in the firing, then popped over the top of the barricade and returned fire in rapid succession.

The first 230-grain hardball punched through the closest gunman's chest, his heart exploding with the force of the Magnum round. The second boattail slug immediately followed, dropping the next gunman in line before he'd expended a dozen rounds from his Steyr. The Chinese gunner was slammed against the side of the panel truck, and fell to the pavement like a stone.

Bolan was tracking on a third gunner when his target suddenly pitched forward and landed face first on the ground. The soldier's attention turned toward the source of a pistol shot, barely audible over the automatic-weapons fire. Jack Grimaldi offered cover fire while hugging the corner of the customs building.

What the hell was Grimaldi doing? The driver was clear of Kaufmann's car with his hostage, and Grimaldi was supposed to be concentrating on getting the car around back and loading the crate. Bolan then realized the ploy. The other three hardmen now had their attention on the pilot, and it was all the edge the Executioner needed. He stood and took careful aim. The Desert Eagle bucked in Bolan's hands, his .44 Magnum rounds ripping flesh and bone from the gunmen. Two more fell under Bolan's crack marksmanship, and the remaining man broke cover and ran for the passenger's door of the panel truck.

As the gunman was running for the truck, the guard from the vestibule now exited the building, drawing his side arm and ordering the gunman to halt. Bolan gritted his teeth and raised his pistol. He sighted on the gunman, but it was too late. The Asian whirled and triggered his weapon, his Parabellum rounds ripping through the luckless security officer.

Bolan continued his cover fire as Grimaldi rushed to Kaufmann's vehicle, but he missed his target by a fraction of an inch. A moment later, the engine was engaged and Grimaldi was powering the hatchback around the corner of the building. Bolan fired several more warning shots for show as the driver climbed aboard, pushing the woman ahead of him. She sat in the center of the truck's bench seat, sandwiched between her two captors.

As the panel truck raced from the scene, Bolan sprinted

for the customs building. He hugged the smooth stone of the building, waiting for Grimaldi to pick him up. He knelt and checked the bullet-riddled guard for a pulse. Dead. Another innocent felled by the menace of terrorism.

Mack Bolan could find some solace—the first phase of his plan had been executed with success.

14

"Everything go okay?" Bolan asked Grimaldi.

"Came off without a hitch," he replied, jerking his thumb to the crate in the rear.

Grimaldi entered the autobahn, accelerating the car to make good distance from the airport. He had obtained the weapons by showing the receipt to the custodian, speaking only in grunts and nods, and looking as official as possible. Kaufmann had given him her extra badge before the mission, which added to his convincing performance as a BND agent.

Bolan leaned his head back and closed his eyes, concentrating on the next phase of his plan. Kaufmann's radio was designed to send a directional signal that they could triangulate with a special receiver mounted in the car between the front seats. Bolan opened his eyes and insured they were receiving a strong signal, then pulled a grid map from his pocket to confirm her location in the panel truck.

As planned, the enemy vehicle was headed south, a mile or two ahead of Bolan and Grimaldi on the same road.

"What kind of equipment did you bring, anyway?" he asked.

Grimaldi smiled. "Oh, now, that's going to make you happy, Sarge. Cowboy was right on the mark with that one. He packed a couple of LAWs, about 240 ounces of plastique and an M-16/M-203 with somewhere on the average of 300 rounds of ball ammunition. The launcher has about twenty grenades. High explosive mixed with a few incendiary.''

''Perfect. Anything else?''

''There's also two .45s in there, and a couple of other things I can't remember.'' There was a wicked glint in Grimaldi's eye. ''Enough to start a little war.''

''Yeah, sounds like just enough,'' Bolan said. ''Jack, you realize that we're going to need to make every attempt to get that plane into friendly hands. Think you know enough about this thing to fly it?''

''Sure thing, buddy. But what about Krizova? Didn't you say he planned to destroy it?''

''If it comes to that, yeah. My primary concern is to get his daughter out. It looks as if these men are going to lead us right to these training grounds you told me about.''

Grimaldi nodded, concentrating on the road, and Bolan began to run down his options. Much of his plan depended on assumption, a fact the Executioner preferred to consider instinct. It was only a slight hope that Kaufmann would be taken to wherever Mila was being held. Once that was confirmed, she would signal Bolan, and he would initiate phase two. Once the women were in the clear, he could take out Schleyer's main force.

It wasn't a complete resolution, but Bolan was counting on it to delay Schleyer's plans, and cause the remnants of the Iron Skull to respond in kind and attempt to hurry the operation. Forcing their timetable would likely cause them to make sloppy mistakes. Bolan hoped it was enough to give him the upper hand—then he would finish the job on their underground hangar.

The other factor to consider was attempting to get word to Stony Man, although Bolan couldn't bring himself to communicate mere assumptions. The U.S. military could go on alert, but without more information, the effort would be futile. The Pacific islands were numerous and remote.

Bolan knew the President didn't have enough faith in him to launch a major mobilization on pure speculation. The objective was now clear. Bolan would have to spearhead an offensive right there and head off the operation before it could get under way.

JÜTTA KAUFMANN FORCED herself to remain calm as she rode with her captors through the main gate posted at the access road to Schleyer's castle. At first, she hadn't been completely happy with the plan to infiltrate the fortress in this manner, but she had ultimately agreed to do it. It would definitely put her within striking distance of Dortmund Linger, regardless if she found Mila Krizova.

At worst, she would gladly sacrifice herself if it meant getting Linger while simultaneously securing the safety of her country and the German people.

Despite her reticence, Kaufmann understood Belasko's mission. She was sympathetic to his cause, and well aware of the effective methods by which he propelled that cause. He was truly one of the most selfless men she had ever encountered, or probably ever would. There was just something about him...something animal, but something pure and good, as well. She admired his tenacity, and his talent as a soldier and warrior. The two of them weren't that much unlike each other when it came to a sense of duty. Nevertheless, Kaufmann had made a promise to Gerhard, and she couldn't compromise her mission—her honor was as much on the line as her life. Linger would have to be eliminated, one way or another, and nothing could stand in the way of that goal.

The panel truck rumbled up to the front of the castle doors, and four uniformed soldiers with Uzi machine pistols encircled the cab. The Asian driver had quickly frisked the woman, and confiscated her pistol, which was now tucked in his waistband. She hoped fate would smile on her, and that would be the only search conducted. If they found the radio microphone and transmitter up her sleeve, the plan would fall apart.

The driver snapped something quickly in his own language, pulling the pistol from his waistband and ordering her down. She couldn't understand him, but the meaning was clear. Kaufmann considered the oddity of the situation. The men from the truck were Asian, but the armed soldiers all appeared European, in one way or another. She didn't know who the Asians were, or why they would be involved with the Iron Skull.

A moment later, it didn't really make a difference. Without warning, the four guards opened fire simultaneously and killed the two Asians without a second thought. Kaufmann jumped back, startled at the sudden and seemingly unprovoked brutality of the act. Both corpses collapsed to the ground, even before the echo of the autofire had died.

One of the guards stepped forward and grabbed her arm, squeezing it hard enough to make her yelp with pain. The man shoved her in the direction of the castle entrance, commanding her to walk ahead of him. Kaufmann shuddered as she felt the warm muzzle of the machine pistol pressed against the small of her back. One false move would doubtless get her killed. Linger probably wouldn't care, but she was certain Edel Schleyer had other plans.

Belasko had surmised that Schleyer wouldn't kill her. She was the businessman's only link to finding the American, and that alone made her a valuable prize. That didn't mean she wouldn't undergo a terrible ordeal at the hands of Schleyer and his men, if the earlier treatment of Belasko was any indication to their habits with all prisoners.

They marched her through what appeared to be a large courtyard filled with various stone statues, exotic plants and a fountain. Under other circumstances, the castle would have been elegant and beautiful, but the gargoyles looked ominous in the flickering torchlight. The group continued through a metal door, two men walking ahead and two behind as they led her up a winding staircase.

Kaufmann was winded by the time they reached their destination. Two guards snapped to attention, and the leader ordered them to open a door behind them, which looked as if it were constructed from pure steel. The men squeezed together on the narrow landing to make room for Kaufmann to pass. She stepped cooperatively through the doorway into the darkened interior, but it didn't seem to make a difference. The contemptuous leader shoved her anyway, and she skinned her hands and knees on the rough stone of the prison floor.

The door closed, shutting out most of the light and clanging loudly before Kaufmann could regain her feet. She rose and stared at the door, trying to conjure an image of how the abusive man would look with a bullet hole between his eyes. She calmed immediately, chastising herself for losing control. There was nothing she could do about it, and keeping her head was vital if their plan was to succeed. She had agreed to do this, and she would just have to accept whatever might come.

The sound of someone moaning softly startled her.

Kaufmann spun on her heel, crouching and taking a defensive martial-arts posture. The source of the moaning hardly posed a threat. In the dim light streaming from the parapet far overhead, she could make out the face of a young woman. It was difficult to guess her age through the cuts, abrasions and bruises. She had long dark hair, which had probably been silky and well groomed at some earlier time. The woman's lips were swollen and cracked, and there were multiple bruises along her forehead, around her eyes and on the point of her chin. The jawbone appeared slightly deformed, and the once-beautiful, dark eyes were now sunken with defeat as they peered at Kaufmann through swollen slits.

"Mein Gott," the woman whispered.

She moved closer to the young woman, who raised her hands in a halfhearted gesture of defense, but they fell quickly. She had been beaten into submission, and the marks were indicative the striking objects had been a man's fists. Kaufmann was stunned at the woman's appearance, but she quickly regained her wits. There was almost no question she was looking at Mila Krizova.

"Sprechen Sie Deutsche?" Kaufmann asked.

Krizova attempted a half smile and held up her thumb and index finger to indicate a minuscule amount. *"Veynich,"* she finally managed to say.

"What about English?"

"Yes, I do speak English," Mila replied weakly. "It is a second language in my country."

"Then we will speak this, since I do not speak Czech," Kaufmann said with a soft laugh. "May I assume you are Mila?"

Krizova nodded. "How did you know?"

"It wasn't too hard to guess this," she said, kneeling next to the young woman. She was sprawled on a stone slab that had served as her bed for what Kaufmann assumed had to have seemed an eternity. "Why have they done this to you?"

"It is not me they care about—it is only my father. I do not know who these men are, but their leader became very angry when I was caught trying to escape. This man is a horrible animal. I am not sure how long I have been here."

"You and your father disappeared nearly a month ago," Kaufmann said slowly, allowing the young woman to take the information in gradually. "This man you are talking about is Edel Schleyer. He is a very powerful man in my country, and he is forcing your father to build him a prototype of the jet fighter.''

"Who are you?" Krizova asked, swallowing hard.

"My name is Jütta Kaufmann. I work for German intelligence, and I am here to get you out of this place. I have a radio, and I will call my friends who are on the outside of the castle. They are going to come and take us out of here. Soon, you will be safe, but you must be patient right now. Can you hold up for just a little more time?"

"I will wait," Krizova confirmed. "I knew help would come."

"Then you must rest for now. We will be gone from here soon."

WHILE DORTMUND LINGER oversaw the removal of the wrecked limousine from the launch tunnel, Schleyer busied himself with Krizova and overseeing the construction of the fighter. Mike Belasko's interference had seriously jeopardized the timetable. Linger had ordered security doubled, which took personnel from the work crews. Schleyer had objected at first, but he realized the need for an uninterrupted operation took precedence over any further delays. Completion of the fighter was paramount to their success. They could ill afford another fiasco.

As Schleyer watched the men at work, he considered the problems ahead. Linger seemed confident the assault could proceed, even with depletion of their ground forces. Soon, the fighter would be finished, Belasko and his allies would be dead and they could continue with their plans to invade Oahu. The success of their operation hinged primarily on the ability of Krizova's fighter to do everything the Czech scientist promised it could. There was no margin for error. Everything had been planned to the last detail.

They would launch the fighter on schedule, or heads would roll. Schleyer had invested millions of dollars into the operation, and he wouldn't be defeated. The inheritance for his people was near, provided they suffered no further losses. Schleyer regretted the decision to surround himself with such incompetence. Careless planning bred inefficiency. It seemed as if they had been required to overcome one blasted obstacle after another. Nevertheless, all of that was about to change.

When the fighter was operational, Schleyer would order Linger to tie up the loose ends. Krizova and his daughter would have to die, as well as the CIA idiot, Dan Lincoln. Schleyer couldn't let anyone else find out he'd been paying the man for his service to the cause. Lincoln was just another pawn—a stupid, greedy American who had become too comfortable with his life-style. Such men could create problems for Schleyer, and that was unacceptable.

Belasko was Schleyer's other primary concern. Schleyer wondered how many other operations such as his had been snuffed out by the big American. Acquiring him as an ally was now out of the question. If they didn't eliminate him soon, he would create a whole new set of problems. Schleyer tried to soothe his rattled nerves. His Chinese friends would make sure Belasko didn't succeed in obtaining the weapons smuggled in by the American government. If they failed, then Schleyer would order Lincoln to initiate the alternate plan.

The German businessman was pleased with himself. He knew godhood was founded in the success of preparation for every eventuality. One didn't rise to a higher plane of existence without practicing foreknowledge. Edel Schleyer wasn't a man who bought into messianic ideals. He did strongly believe in reincarnation. When he left this life, he would come back as omnipotent and omnipresent. All powerful. A power that didn't come from stature, or social status, or even money. His power would be spiritual, a power that guided the paths of man, that deposed the physical realm in favor of a new order.

It was Edel Schleyer's inheritance. He deserved this above all else.

Dortmund Linger approached him. "The launch tunnel is clear, and I have a crew patching the damage as we speak."

"Very good, Commander," Schleyer replied with a smile of satisfaction. "Now, if the good doctor can just finish with his end of our bargain, we should be able to launch tomorrow morning."

Schleyer's purposeful statement wasn't lost on Vasec Krizova. He overheard the conversation and peered down from his place in the cockpit frame. A crew was adding the finishing welds to the nose of the fighter, and would soon begin riveting the panels in place.

Krizova stared at the two men with unadulterated disgust and hatred. He'd given up almost all hope his daughter was alive. Schleyer knew Krizova was only operating on a whim that Mila lived. He'd purposely told Krizova that he would execute Mila *if* Krizova didn't finish the fighter on time. Thus far, Schleyer's careful selection of words seemed to be having the desired effect. He was using his leverage against the scientist, and pulling out all the stops in a desperate attempt to make their plan for invasion succeed.

Although his investigation didn't prove the idea credible, Schleyer was still highly suspicious of the fact Krizova might have in some way assisted in Belasko's escape. Next to Schleyer and Linger, Krizova was the only one who knew the compound intimately. The sentries were also familiar with the maze of tunnels leading from the hangar, but there had been no sign of treachery from any of Linger's men to this point. That meant either American or German intelligence had inserted a mole early on, or Krizova had managed to help the American without anyone's knowledge. Schleyer was betting on the latter explanation.

"I think I might have an explanation for Belasko's escape," Linger offered, as if he'd been reading Schleyer's thoughts.

Schleyer didn't take his eyes from Krizova, who had turned his attention back to the work inside the cockpit, as he replied, "How is that, Commander?"

"Two of my men had been facing Belasko's direction during the firefight, but they were shot from behind. The alarms went off because the motion sensors I had installed detected movement near the tunnel entrance. Belasko was nowhere near the doors when they went off, so he could not have triggered them."

"You think he had help," Schleyer concluded for Linger, nodding his understanding.

"Yes," Linger replied. "I am positive of it now. Someone killed those men. Someone other than Belasko. I am guessing it was the American, Grimes, or possibly even Jütta Kaufmann."

"Belasko was captured inside the compound. How could either of these people know the location of this underground complex?"

"A considerable amount of time had passed between his evasion of Gabrielle's ambush and his penetration of the complex. It is altogether possible he told them."

Schleyer stopped to ponder Linger's theory. If outside elements *had* penetrated the complex, they would have needed previous knowledge about the entrance. The infiltrators hadn't gained entrance the same way as Belasko. The information provided him with access through the old U-Bahn tunnels and not the camouflaged entrance. This meant anyone assisting him would have made entry the same way. No, there was no possible way outsiders could have known about the entrance. It had to be an accidental discovery.

"I am more inclined to believe that someone tailed my vehicle to the complex, Commander. That is the only reasonable explanation."

"How could someone have followed you undetected?" Linger pressed.

"That is what I would like to know," Schleyer spit, eyeing Linger with disgust. "Your men were assigned to protect me. Instead, they almost got me killed. They should have known someone was following us. Unless—" Schleyer's voice faltered in midsentence as an idea came to him.

Linger waited expectantly.

"Unless whoever followed us had a unique knowledge of the area."

Linger nodded. "Jütta Kaufmann was raised in that area. It is very possible she followed you."

"If you're right, and the information from your BND contacts is correct about her alliance with this Belasko, it is also possible she has allied herself with Herr Grimes."

"It is more than possible. She aided his escape from the airport, as well as killing two of our men, posted there with police credentials I had forged. My informant told me she was assigned to intercept Grimes and the weapons he was smuggling."

A merc rushed forward and saluted the two men. "Commander, there is a phone call for you."

Linger nodded and excused himself. Schleyer watched with interest as the towering mercenary crossed the complex and took the call. He nodded curtly several times, then returned shortly with an undeniable expression of satisfaction. Schleyer was anxious to hear the news. Judging from Linger's face, it was probably the call about Belasko.

"Your Chinese associates captured only one from the

customs office. Four of them were killed at the scene. Lieutenant Meldric says they met some serious resistance. Belasko and Grimes apparently got away, but they managed to capture Jütta. He also says they eliminated the remaining two upon their arrival at your castle. That will leave no survivors to talk from that end.''

"This is unfortunate," Schleyer said softly, his eyes narrowing to angered slits. "The capture of Kaufmann is something, but it is likely Belasko got away with the weapons.''

"He will launch an offensive against us here. I must go and prepare for his arrival.''

"Not yet, Commander," Schleyer replied. "Our first course of action should be to question Kaufmann. She might have quite a bit of information to give us. I am sure she knows what Belasko has planned. This could be quite useful to us. We must go to the fortress and I will give you the honor of applying your unique talents. I'm sure that will satisfy your appetite to clean up this Kaufmann mess once and for all.''

"Who will supervise the operation here?''

"I should think your new executive officer can handle that.''

"Very well, sir.''

"Give him his instructions and meet me at the tunnel entrance. We will depart in five minutes. I will contact Gabrielle and order her to return, as well.''

"It shall be as you wish," Linger said. He performed a slight bow, then set off to find his second-in-command.

As Schleyer turned and headed for the phone, he murmured, "Yes, it shall.''

15

The Executioner lay flat on the cold hard ground. The sun had disappeared behind a gray cloud cover, casting shadows among the trees of the forest landscape. A storm was brewing, and Bolan couldn't help but muse on that reality. He studied Schleyer's fortress carefully, making occasional notations in a small notebook. Bolan used Grimaldi's compass to shoot azimuths and compute ranges. He had even made a brief sketch of the immediate terrain for later reference. He would need it if Kaufmann's signal came after dark.

Grimaldi sat on a rise behind Bolan, loading clips for the M-16/M-203 combo, and the Colt Government Model pistols. Both men were now attired in camouflage fatigues and combat boots—amenities Stony Man had provided along with the weaponry. Bolan wore his Beretta and Desert Eagle pistols, and one of the tubelike M-72 A-2 light antitank weapons was slung across his back. The LAW was an impressive weapon, capable of huge ranges and weighing less than ten pounds. Infantrymen called the disposable, one-shot weapon the "tank-killer," and with good reason. It fired a high-explosive rocket, capable of blowing holes in armor plating as thick as eight inches, which was more than enough to effectively disable the armored vehicles conducting maneuvers. The priority would be the tank turrets. As long as Bolan could take them out first, his chances for survival and success were increased twentyfold.

The soldier would have preferred to stall his attack until nightfall, but everything was dependent on Kaufmann's signal. She was inside and calling the shots out of pure necessity. He knew he would have to be fully prepared to launch his assault at any moment. Once he had the signal, he would only have about eight minutes to disable the heavy armor, penetrate the compound and rescue the two women.

Bolan jotted another notation, then crawled backward until he had reached Grimaldi, who was finishing his last magazine.

"Satisfied?" the pilot asked.

"I'm never satisfied," Bolan remarked, "but I think I have enough information in the tactical department. How do things look on your end?"

"Last one," Grimaldi noted, gesturing with the 30-round magazine.

Bolan sat on a large rock and patted the LAW casing. "I take it you're familiar with these?"

"Yeah," Grimaldi said, nodding. "Cowboy's emphatic about keeping us current with all the latest weapons. Twice a year we have to get certified on the Farm's range. He usually fits me in with Able Team." Grimaldi laughed. "It's worth going just to see Ironman and Pol go at it."

There was a flash of daylight in Bolan's periphery. He sidled to his previous position, lay prone and brought the binoculars to his eyes. Grimaldi crawled up next to him, a quizzical expression on his face. Without the aid of the binoculars, he couldn't make out the subject of Bolan's interest. It appeared to be a black vehicle rolling up in front of the castle doors.

"What is it?"

Bolan only grunted a reply, then passed the binoculars to his friend. "It's a Hummer. I saw that same vehicle when those Iron Skull troops attacked me and Jütta near the hotel.''

"Anybody important?''

"Linger, I'm guessing. Maybe Schleyer, maybe both.''

"If it is, now's our chance. You could easily hit them with the LAW from here.''

Bolan shook his head emphatically. "No way. We're going to have to wait for Jütta's signal. Besides, we've got one chance to take out those two tanks they've got, and that's one apiece.''

"You're the boss, Sarge," Grimaldi said. "We might not get another chance like this, though.''

"We'll get another chance," Bolan replied. "Trust me.''

SCHLEYER AND LINGER EXITED their armored Hummer and went inside the castle. A lieutenant greeted them at the front doors, snapped a smart salute and escorted the two men to an anteroom off the courtyard.

Scheleyer ordered the two women brought to them. The two men sipped cognac as they waited. When the two women arrived, Schleyer instructed the guards to tie them to the metal chairs. The guards pinned the women's arms to their sides and bound their feet.

"Wait outside," Schleyer said. When the guards were gone, he turned his attention to the BND agent. "Well, my dear, so nice of you to join us.''

"Mr. Schleyer?" she said. "I cannot believe that you are involved with this animal.''

"I am glad to know you think so highly of Commander Linger." Schleyer turned to his colleague, adding, "Did you hear that, Commander? She thinks you are nothing more than a wild beast of the field.''

"I heard," Linger said tightly.

Schleyer returned his attention to the woman. "You have been very meddlesome in the affairs of the Iron Skull. You have also interfered with the construction of the fighter and aided a man who I believe is considered a fugitive by your own superiors. You seem to have difficulty taking orders. Commander Linger feels that you need to be taught a lesson.''

"Torture will do you no good, Schleyer." Kaufmann twisted her left arm just slightly, struggling to free herself from the ropes.

"It would not benefit you to attempt escape," Schleyer stated. "You would not get far, and this area is rugged country."

"I would survive."

"Not if we kill you first," Linger interjected.

"Easy, Commander," Schleyer cautioned. "We must not be premature about this. They will both die slow, painful deaths. All in good time. First, we must know where to find Belasko."

"Belasko will find you, Schleyer," Kaufmann challenged. "When he does, he will destroy you and the Iron Skull. Your plans will fail."

"What do you know of our plans?" Linger asked.

"I know that you intend to attack innocent civilians on American soil. You have butchered hundreds of our own people, and now your thirst for blood extends to the Americans. It will do you no good. Belasko has already set a plan in motion to eliminate your operation for good, and he has notified his government. No doubt they are already prepared for your attack. With any luck, the Americans will blow Dr. Krizova's jet out of the sky before you know it."

"I do not think so," Schleyer said. He nodded to Mila. "I think you should ask your friend what she thinks about her father's fighter. It is the ultimate weapon of war. A paradox to the modern aircraft. It is nearly as fast as a missile, virtually undetectable by radar and capable of things you could not even imagine. We will most certainly succeed."

"What are you hoping to gain?" the German agent pressed.

Schleyer clasped his hands behind him and began pacing the room. "I intend to recompense the evil that has been done to my people. To *our* people, Miss Kaufmann! Since the beginning of the century, the Americans have repressed the right of the German people to expand their culture. We have not been allowed to maintain any kind of standing military, nor to grow as a country. We are quickly running out of space. Jobs are scarce, poverty is high and our children are close to starving. We must expand our horizons. Adolf Hitler called it 'living space.'"

"Adolf Hitler was a genocidal maniac," Kaufmann countered. "Do you intend to start the Fourth Reich?"

"Not at all," Schleyer continued. "Although we do have an inheritance. An inheritance out of which the Americans have repeatedly cheated us. I intend to purge them with fire. I intend to take one of their most precious possessions. We must rebuild the German culture, and the only way to do that is by acquiring the correct materials, and building our military into a war machine unparalleled in the history of all mankind."

"You're delusional."

Schleyer stopped his pacing, walked to the woman, and slapped her across the face. "Shut up, you government bitch! Do you think I will tolerate your obsessive rantings and arguments? Commander Linger, gag her!"

Linger immediately took one of the white linen napkins from a nearby table and obeyed the order. Kaufmann struggled against the gag, but Linger was very strong. He pulled the napkin against her mouth, and the rough linen bit at the corners. Linger tied the ends of the napkin behind her, then belted her across the back of the head brutally. The blow nearly knocked her unconscious.

"Pay attention, whore," Linger said.

Schleyer continued as calmly as he had begun. "Now then, as I was saying? Oh, yes…the invasion will succeed.

Dr. Krizova's fighter has the ability to engage multiple targets from many miles away. We will strike at Oahu's military base, known to the Americans as Diamond Head. This will result in an unbelievable acquisition of material. Enough to build a fleet of planes just like Dr. Krizova's prototype. We will then build an army of well-trained pilots, and conquer the Americans on their own soil. Those who wish to show their subservience to the Iron Skull's elite military will be allowed to live. Those who do not will be destroyed."

The door opened and Gabrielle Reinmaul entered. *"Guten tag, meine liebe,"* she greeted Schleyer.

"Ah, Gabrielle. I am glad to see you again." Schleyer kissed her, then gestured to Kaufmann. "I believe you know Jütta Kaufmann of the BND."

Reinmaul leaned close to the woman and smiled coldly. "Yes, I do remember her. This is the bitch who escaped from my men. It is so good to see you again. I shall enjoy watching you die."

"Commander Linger, I have a few things of business to which I must attend. You may begin your interrogation of Jütta Kaufmann. Make sure you find out everything she knows about Mike Belasko, and where we can find him. I would appreciate it if you let Gabrielle assist you." Schleyer looked at Kaufmann, a satisfactory smile crossing his lips. "I am sure it will prove to be most educational. And kill this Czech bitch. We have no further use for her."

"As you wish," Linger replied.

Mila's eyes widened, and she struggled to free herself. Kaufmann turned her gaze to the young woman and shook her head helplessly. The meaning seemed clear. If she struggled, they would only kill her sooner to prevent her from becoming a nuisance. Mila ceased her gyrations, and Kaufmann looked forward, not meeting Schleyer's smug glance.

When Schleyer had departed, Linger removed her gag. Gabrielle sat on the edge of the table and lit a cigarette.

She watched with interest as Linger sized up their old nemesis, walking around the two women and staring hard at them. She couldn't have cared less about Krizova, but Jütta Kaufmann was another story. She, Kaufmann and Linger had all been associates once in the BND. It would be thrilling but simultaneously a shame to see Kaufmann die. Linger was especially talented when it came to obtaining information.

"I am very disappointed in you, Jütta," Linger said. "I thought I had trained you better than this. You should have not betrayed me. However, your crimes against me are not nearly as severe as those against the cause. Many of my men, *good* men, have died because of you."

"And how many good people have died because of you, Dortmund?" she asked.

"This is the cost of doing business," Linger said with a shrug. "I cannot help what happens to other people. If they were not for us, then we had to assume they were against us. Either that, or they simply outlived their usefulness to the Iron Skull."

"I know you well, Dortmund, remember?" Kaufmann said. "You don't really believe in Edel Schleyer's cause."

"What I believe doesn't matter," Linger replied. "I owe a lot to Edel Schleyer. He rewards loyalty, and so I am loyal. You are not loyal, Jütta. I thought you understood my motivations well enough to know why I am doing this. It is not because I enjoy it, believe me. I do this out of necessity. No war can be won through mere attrition. War is won through killing your enemy. You should understand that. Your friend Belasko understands that."

"He has nothing to do with this."

"Oh, I think he has everything to do with it. Which brings me to the point. Where is Belasko, and what are his plans?"

"Do you honestly believe I will tell you anything, Dortmund?" Kaufmann asked. The tone in her voice registered her incredulity.

"No, I do not. Actually, that is too bad for you. This could have been easy for you. Now, we must do things the hard way."

Linger stepped forward and yanked Kaufmann's shirt front over her face. He tore the bra she was wearing from her chest, exposing her breasts. Linger walked over to the table and pulled a long candle from one of the holders, then ordered Reinmaul to light it. Krizova began to scream, rocking in her chair and trying to escape her bonds. Linger walked back to where the women were seated and kicked the young woman in the stomach. She gasped for breath, her screams turning into sobs as Linger held the candle close to one of Kaufmann's nipples.

The woman trembled as she felt the heat applied to the sensitive area. She braced herself, twisting her left wrist again.

"Tell me what I want to know, Jütta," Linger whispered. "Do not let it come to this. Do not make it hard for yourself. You have no allegiance to Belasko."

Reinmaul watched the action, smiling and smoking her cigarette calmly.

"Tell me where Belasko is, eh?" Linger said, his voice dropping even more. "Where is he?"

Linger moved the candle closer.

"Where is he?" the merc leader shouted. "Tell me! Tell me!"

A muffled explosion sounded from somewhere outside the compound.

"What the hell was that?" Reinmaul asked.

Linger's head snapped up, and he instantly knew Kaufmann didn't have to answer his question. Even as the first sounds of machine-gun fire reached their ears, and the sirens sounded all over the castle, it was obvious where Belasko was at—he was right under their noses.

"Gabrielle!" Linger called. "Take these two back to the tower. I must find Schleyer and organize the men."

"*Jawohl.*"

Linger departed through the door, ordering the guards to follow him. Reinmaul stepped forward and began to untie the BND agent. She was careful to hold on to the woman with one hand, keeping the slip knot engaged around Kaufmann's right wrist as she untied the left. When the rope fell away, a black cord with a small gold screen dislodged from under the agent's sleeve and fell to the stone floor.

Reinmaul's eyes widened in surprise. She bent to retrieve the small device, then traced the wire up under Kaufmann's sleeve. She could barely contain her horror. It appeared to be some kind of transmitter. Reinmaul yanked the cord down and away, bringing several strips of adhesive tape with it. She yanked the agent's shirt down and held the microphone dangling from a frayed wire.

"What is this?" Reinmaul demanded.

Kaufmann swung her right arm over her head and brought it forward, spinning the woman in front. Tendons gave in Reinmaul's wrist, and she realized her mistake even as her knees hit the cold, hard stone. She had wrapped her hand around the prisoner's rope, and it had been the perfect leverage Kaufmann needed to take her down. The BND agent brought her left fist crashing down on a nerve in Reinmaul's neck, and the blow knocked her unconscious.

Struggling to catch her breath, Kaufmann pulled the ropes from her feet, untied Krizova, who was still sobbing with the aftershock of almost witnessing Linger's bizarre torture methods.

"Come on, Mila," the woman urged gently. "We're getting out of here."

16

If Dortmund Linger really wanted to know where Bolan was, the Executioner had no qualms about telling him.

He sent his message in the form of the first LAW rocket. The explosive shell struck home, blowing the huge gun barrel completely off one of the tanks and melting part of the turret. Bolan tossed the LAW shell aside and sprinted down a hill to the perimeter fence. Mercenaries positioned across the compound were running wildly in all directions. Apparently, none of them had seen where the rocket originated, and nobody had noticed Bolan.

The soldier tossed a piece of metal strapping from the LAW at the fence. No sparks showered up. He listened closely over the ruckus and didn't detect a humming noise. A roll of razor-sharp concertina wire topped the fence, but it was safe to assume the wire wasn't electrified. Bolan inserted a blasting cap and dual wire into a small amount of C-4, and attached the other two ends of the wire to posts of a manual detonator. He ran back, extending the length of wire, and dropped behind the rut at the bottom of the hill. Bolan keyed up his radio.

"Now, Jack!"

The Executioner squeezed the charging handle of the detonator several times as the other LAW rocket launched from the tree line two hundred yards to his right. The fence gave in at the same time as the turret on the second tank—which had just begun to move—exploded. The immense heat of the LAW rocket ignited the charged shell inside the tank, and both explosions sent deadly shards of superheated metal flying in all directions. Unfortunately for the enemy, several men near the tank went up with their metal monstrosity.

Bolan dived through the torn fencing and angled toward the castle, popping a 40 mm grenade into the M-203 on the run. A group of five mercenaries finally noticed the Executioner and took off to intercept him. But he spotted them first and triggered his M-203 from the waist. The HE grenade struck just in front of the group. Limbs flew in every direction as the grenade detonated, and the remainder of the bodies toppled into the large crater left in its wake.

The soldier snapped the selector lever on the M-16 to full-auto, then dropped and rolled as an armored half track bore down on him. A merc in the vehicle stood on the front seat of the open-air passenger's compartment, shooting Uzi rounds over the rim of the windshield. Another was positioned in the rear storage compartment, assisting his cohort with an HK-21E machine gun mounted to the vehicle. Bolan sighted on the machine gunner and stroked the trigger. A hail of 5.56 mm rounds tore through the terrorist's belly and chest as the vehicle passed, and he sailed over the far edge of the half track.

Bolan regained his feet and fired another salvo before the driver could bring the half track completely around. The Uzi-toting merc flipped up and out of the vehicle, his Uzi clattering off the hood. The driver gunned the engine, trying to run down the Executioner, but Bolan rolled away again, getting to his feet and firing as the driver passed his line of sight. The soldier was on the move even as his rounds struck the driver, running parallel to the slowing half track until he had gained access to the vehicle.

Bolan hauled the corpse of the driver from behind the wheel and tossed him off the side. He stood on the accelerator and swung the half track in the direction of the castle doors. Risking a quick glance behind him, he saw Grimaldi crash through the front gate of the compound. He could barely see the pilot's arm out the front window, squeezing off shots with one of the Colt Government Model pistols Kissinger had provided.

Grimaldi was one of the bravest men he'd ever known. He was responsible for planting the charges along specific points in the castle exterior, and Bolan knew he could count on the man to do the job right, despite the enormous odds. Grimaldi was no demolitions expert, but he could follow simple directions. Bolan didn't have to worry about the ace pilot.

The Executioner triggered his M-16 again, emptying his first clip as he fired on a pair of mercs approaching the half track on his left flank. The 5.56 mm tumblers ripped through the men's bodies like air-gun pellets through rice paper. They staggered around for several seconds like string-controlled puppets before collapsing to the ground.

Bolan made the castle's front doors and charged the M-203 with an incendiary grenade. He went EVA on the passenger's side and took cover behind the half track as a squad of six mercs exited the castle and began to fan out. The leader stopped them short with a raised hand, and stared at the half track in puzzlement. Bolan used the hesitancy to his advantage, popping over the lip of the passenger's door and pulling the trigger of the M-203. The butt of the M-16 kicked against his shoulder with the force of a 16-gauge shotgun. He ducked behind the half track as the incendiary round struck the steel frame of the front doors and exploded. White-hot flame instantly incinerated the four closest gunmen, raining a shower of burning phosphorous onto tender flesh. The men began to scream as they watched their flesh burn. The two survivors were still scrambling to recover as Bolan popped a fresh clip into his M-16.

He dispatched the remaining pair with a quick burst of autofire.

A storm of 9 mm rounds chewed up the cobblestoned path around the soldier's feet, and others ricocheted off the armored half track. Bolan whirled to see a group of terrorists approaching on the run, trailed by a Hummer. He slung his M-16 and backstepped into the half track. He vaulted the seat, took up a position behind the HK-21E and squeezed the trigger. The weapon rocked against his shoulder as Bolan selectively fired corkscrew bursts across the human wave of terrorists.

The Heckler & Koch machine gun was a versatile weapon, with origins dating back to 1970. A burst of 7.62 mm NATO rounds spit from the barrel at a cyclic rate of 900 rounds per minute. Bolan's first target was the Hummer gunner, positioned behind his own HK-21E. The man's body was torn apart by the heavy rounds that struck him. He staggered backward and landed with a dull thud in the back of the Hummer.

Bolan swept the weapon down on the approaching gunmen. The Iron Skull terrorists dived for cover, some taking the NATO rounds as they attempted to evade the deadly barrage. The HK-21E's air-cooled barrel became red as Bolan gunned down one gunner after another in a ceaseless onslaught of gunfire. The Hummer rolled to a halt, then moved forward again, simply driving over the bodies stacking up in front of it. One man managed to escape Bolan's fire, sweeping around and trying to outflank him.

Bolan saw the man and let the M-16 slide off his shoulder. He inserted the weapon between himself and the machine-gun mount and squeezed the trigger. His initial burst missed the gunman by inches, but he immediately followed with a second burst. The 5.56 mm rounds struck their target, punching through the man's legs and head, spinning him away. Bolan used his left hand to trigger the HK-21E again, careful to keep his arm clear of the belt. The Hummer's windshield imploded, raining glass on the occupants inside. Bolan fired another salvo to finish the job.

As he ceased firing, his attention was drawn to a man across the compound issuing orders to a group of seasoned troops and pointing in Bolan's direction. The men piled into the back of an armored personnel carrier mounted with a .50-caliber Browning, and the diesel engine roared to life. The APC moved toward him, and Bolan knew he was better off inside the castle.

He dropped from the back of the half track and quickly moved to the castle doors. Bolan peered inside the torchlit courtyard, his M-16/M-203 held at the ready. No resistance greeted him. The place looked deserted, but Bolan knew there were troops inside. Mythical statues loomed overhead, peppering the courtyard like sentries from ancient days.

It smelled like an ambush, but the soldier was more comfortable against stone statues than an APC filled with angry terrorists. Bolan moved along the inside wall, crouching in the shadows. A score of doors dotted the circular walls, each one a mystery. It seemed to him as if Schleyer were calling out to him, taunting him to select a door and find out what was behind it.

Bolan paused to tap the radio earpiece. There had still been no signal from Kaufmann. He had launched his attack for her sake. Most of the conversation hadn't been audible, but Bolan had caught enough to know that she was in trouble. When Linger had demanded to know where Bolan was, and Bolan could hear Krizova screaming, that was all he needed. His decision to launch the assault might have been premature, but there was no reason to start second-guessing himself now. Where was she? Had the transmitter been discovered?

There was no need for guesswork in the next second.

A score of armed mercs appeared through a door on the far side of the courtyard. Bolan went prone and triggered his M-16. The first two in line dropped before their counterparts realized they should take cover. For troops who had been training as long as these, Bolan had taken note of their disorganization. It was obvious to the warrior that many of his enemy had never faced combat.

Bolan drew another grenade from the waist satchel and popped it into the M-203. He aimed at a gargoyle statue above the hiding troops and fired. The 40 mm HE round sailed through the courtyard in a graceful arc and struck the base of the statue. It exploded on impact and dumped hundreds of pounds of stone onto the unwary troops, crushing several beneath the weight. The remaining gunners broke cover and spread out, trying to flank Bolan.

The Executioner popped in another HE grenade, then stroked the M-16's trigger, spitting rounds at two soldiers circling on the right. Bolan's aim was true, and the M-16's tumbler rounds slammed into the terrorists and threw them against the courtyard wall. He swung the M-203 toward the remaining three gunners flanking him on the left, dropping the grenade in the dead center of the group. Their bodies flew apart as the heated shrapnel tore through flesh and the concussion lifted them off the ground.

The courtyard clear of troops, Bolan sprinted across the elaborate expanse to one of the far doors. Since he was out of communication with Kaufmann, he would have to conduct a room-by-room search. The first door he entered opened up into a darkened great hall of some kind. In the dim lighting that spilled through the open door, he could see no other exits. One down.

Bolan backed out of the room, leaving the door open. As he considered his next move, the sound of feet on stone attracted his attention. The men from the APC were now pouring in through the entrance doors. Bolan crouched and loaded a grenade as six men spread out in the courtyard. The soldier triggered his M-16, spraying the enemy with autofire. He beelined for cover near a stone staircase jutting from the inside wall of a parapet, firing to keep heads down as he did.

Reaching the round staircase, he fired the 40 mm grenade, but the shot was high, blowing chunks of refurbished stone in every direction. Bolan cursed as he ascended the stone steps. He fired on the run, reaching a door at the top, which was locked. He launched a kick below the lock, and the wooden door caved inward. The Executioner forged ahead, sweeping the muzzle of the M-16 in all directions. He was in an empty circular room, with another door visible on the far side. Edel Schleyer apparently had a fetish for mazes, and it was becoming increasingly difficult for Bolan to keep his bearings. He crossed the room and tried the door. The handle turned smoothly, and he entered into an interior circular staircase.

Bolan descended the steps three at a time. The enemy had the advantage at this point. They knew the layout of the castle better than he did, and the soldier was cognizant of the fact his luck wasn't going to hold forever. He reached the bottom of the stairs and pushed through a third door, stepping onto a landing that led in opposing directions. Bolan took the right hallway, moving away from the terrorist army chasing him. His offense was quickly becoming a defense, and he needed something to turn the tables.

And where was Kaufmann?

As if in answer, Bolan rounded the corner of the corridor and bumped into her and a young dark-haired woman who had obviously been beaten severely. It had to be Mila Krizova. Kaufmann threw her arms around Bolan, but he gruffly detached himself from the beautiful BND agent.

"No time for happy reunions," he growled. He turned

to the dark-haired woman standing next to Kaufmann. "Are you Mila?"

"Yes," she said. "You are Mike Belasko, yes?"

"Yes. Do you know another way out of here?"

"Have you tried the courtyard?" she asked.

"No dice." The sound of boots running along the stone floors reached his ears. "They're coming. Go!"

He handed Kaufmann his Beretta 93-R, then pushed the women ahead of him. The trio sprinted down the corridor, the BND agent in the lead, then Krizova, with Bolan as the rear guard. They passed an adjoining hallway which dead-ended at a door, and Bolan backed the group up and directed them to move down the corridor. The two women obeyed without hesitation. The threesome reached the door, and Bolan shouldered past them. He opened the door and peered out. It was the courtyard. The front door was only guarded by two men.

The Executioner stepped through the doorway and raised the M-16 to his shoulder. He couldn't afford to miss, and he didn't. The sentries fell to the ground, drilled by the volley of 5.56 mm rounds. Bolan scanned both directions and stepped into the open. He didn't notice a door opening above them until it was too late. Kaufmann yelled a warning a heartbeat before she shoved him out of the line of fire.

Bolan twisted toward the sound of gunfire, even as the multiple 9 mm rounds from her pistol cored through the woman's lithe frame. Her body jerked in spasms as she was hammered into the open door by the force of the gunfire. Bolan recognized the shooter by the figure alone, even as the Desert Eagle filled his fist and tracked on the target.

Bolan squeezed the trigger.

The 230-grain Magnum slug crossed the expanse in less than one-tenth of second, punching through Gabrielle Reinmaul's chest and lifting her off the ground. The woman's head slammed against the stone wall behind her, breaking her neck as she went down. Bolan lowered the barrel of the big .44 slowly after he detected no further movement. He holstered his weapon and turned toward Kaufmann's bullet-riddled body.

Blood mixed with pink, frothy sputum spewed from her mouth, running down the sides of her jaw. She coughed, wheezing for breath as Bolan knelt beside her. She looked at the warrior with glazed eyes, but he saw no fear there. She smiled, nodding assurance that she didn't consider her death in vain. She whispered something to him, something he couldn't quite make out, and then died quietly in his arms. Bolan had caught only one word. *Linger.* The sensation of unmitigated revenge burned in Bolan's heart as he disentangled himself from Jütta Kaufmann's broken, lifeless body.

Bolan picked up the Beretta and handed it to Krizova. His ice-blue eyes studied the frightened woman expectantly. There was a tremble in the petite hand that reached out to take the oversize pistol from him.

"You know how to use this?" Bolan hissed.

"I—I have never f-fired a gun," the young woman stammered.

"You point the barrel at anything that moves, other than me, and squeeze the trigger. Got it?"

"I th-think so."

"Lets move out."

Bolan took the lead, M-16 held low as he sprinted for the door. A series of nearby explosions rocked the castle. Jack Grimaldi had pulled it off. Now it was time to move on. They reached the doorway, and the soldier found the half track right where he'd left it. He gestured for Krizova to climb in as the sound of movement behind them signaled new arrivals.

The Executioner turned and hugged the doorframe,

spraying the interior of the courtyard with short, controlled bursts of gunfire. Merc after merc poured into the courtyard, only to fall under the merciless onslaught of Bolan's unswerving marksmanship. He emptied the M-16's clip, popped in a fresh one and dispatched several more terrorists before climbing into the cab of the half track and cranking the engine to life.

"Mind if I tag along?" a voice called behind him.

Bolan turned to see Grimaldi standing in the back of the vehicle next to the HK-21E, smiling with devilish satisfaction.

"Drive for the gates," Bolan said.

"Where's Jütta?" he asked as they traded places.

When Bolan didn't answer, Grimaldi's expression became filled with sadness. The pilot spun the half track wordlessly, moving toward the exit at a breakneck pace. Bolan fired on the remnants of the Iron Skull trying to mobilize for a fresh encounter with the Executioner, taking out carefully selected targets.

During a break in the firing, Grimaldi called to Bolan. The soldier turned his head to see the pilot gesturing at an APC blocking the gates ahead, mercenaries lying prone in front of it, others using the bulky troop carrier as cover. Bolan abandoned his machine gun and loaded a smoke grenade. He aimed high, launching the grenade into an arc. He followed it with a second as Grimaldi narrowed the gap. That would provide their escape cover. Bolan retrieved a third 40 mm casing of HE and fired straight ahead.

The APC erupted into smoke and flame, metal shrapnel tearing into several troops on the ground. One large chunk from the engine cover of the APC decapitated a man attempting to escape the secondary explosions from Bolan's assault.

The Executioner slung his weapon and returned to manning the machine gun. He followed troop movements with the weapon, alternately swinging the barrel to either side of any target that presented itself. The terrorists were flung in every direction. One stray round nicked Bolan's hand, but he barely felt the pain as he depressed the trigger in sustained bursts.

Bolan almost lost his balance as Grimaldi swerved around the smoking shell of the APC blocking their path. The pilot smashed the half track through the front fence as Bolan aimed toward one remaining soldier tracking on the vehicle with an M-79 grenade launcher. A flash of recognition crossed the mercenary's face a moment before his head blew apart. Bolan had caught the same glimpse, causing only a momentary hesitation. It had been the young man he'd encountered at the riverside shed.

Another young life had been wasted that day.

Bolan ceased his firing, checking the rear for stragglers as Grimaldi passed through the cover of smoke and emerged onto the road leading from the compound. Even from that distance, the soldier could make out the gaping holes left in the huge castle fortress. It was ironic that such a beautiful piece of historical architecture had housed men determined to carry out such a horrible task.

Nevertheless, Bolan had delivered a telling blow to the Iron Skull. Many of their vehicles were still intact, but he wasn't worried. He had already planned for that problem. If they could successfully get the fighter off the ground, Bolan would make sure Grimaldi came back to finish that business once and for all. With Mila Krizova safe, the final phase of the operation could commence.

Bolan took a deep breath and pushed thoughts of Jütta Kaufmann from his mind. He needed to concentrate on the task at hand. Their escape was in the bag, but Edel Schleyer had invested too much in his plans to quit now. He would attempt to salvage the operation—he was predictable in that respect. The man was insane, and Bolan fully intended to put him down for eternity. As long as Schleyer lived, the threat of the Iron Skull lived. Therefore, Schleyer was next on the Executioner's agenda.

And so was Dortmund Linger.

17

Commander Dortmund Linger viewed the smoking carnage across the battlefield and let out a snort of disgust.

Everywhere he looked, his troops lay dead or wounded. The dozen or so remaining men assigned to the compound carried their comrades to waiting vehicles for transport to the makeshift infirmary set up inside the castle. Belasko's assault had left nearly everything in their mobile arsenal unsalvageable. Maybe a half-dozen vehicles were still operational. The half tracks had been staged in the center of the grounds to serve as ambulances, while three APCs conducted roving patrols along the perimeter.

The castle was remote enough that they could expect no outside interference. There were no police nearby, and the nearest military installation—or what could pass for one—was in Frankfurt. The countryside was as barren as the morale of Linger's mercenary force. Death and suffering was nothing new to Linger. He'd experienced plenty in his travels. His men had truly been loyal. Although many were inexperienced, they hadn't run from the attackers. That would have been the ultimate defeat.

Belasko was a scourge to the Iron Skull. He was one man. One man had done this! In one respect, Linger admired the American. They were very much alike—both soldiers who fought passionately for their beliefs. The difference came in the fact Belasko didn't have a worthless orb of steel tying him down. Linger now considered Edel

Schleyer a punishment forced upon him by a merciless deity. The god of war had hung Schleyer around Linger's neck like a cumbersome chunk of iron ore.

Instead of leading his troops in battle, Linger had foolishly risked defeat by attempting to protect Schleyer. Linger's great stone god had become nothing more than a soft and lowly slug. Men like Schleyer weren't worth the talents of men like Linger. There was no amount of money that could buy a man of Linger's caliber, no inheritance deserving of his bravery and dedication. The only cause Dortmund Linger intended to serve from this point forward was the one he deemed most important at the time. However, Linger knew he had no one to blame but himself. He had brought this sad affair upon his own head.

It was a mistake he meant to correct.

Linger turned and marched inside the fortress. Two men hovering over a body near the door leading to the barracks called for his attention. Linger strolled to where the men stood and gazed at the subject of their interest. Jütta Kaufmann was sprawled across the broken remains of a gargoyle statue. Bullet holes were scattered across her chest and abdomen, and dried blood mixed with saliva covered her face.

Linger could only shake his head. There was just a twinge of remorse. Despite their differences, Linger noted the fact Jütta Kaufmann had died with honor. To forfeit life in combat was the ultimate test of a warrior. That thought brought a smile to Linger's face. She had died honorably, because he had trained her honorably. Her death would probably torment Belasko for the few hours he had remaining in his life.

"Take the body outside and burn it," Linger said. "Make sure everyone has an unobstructed view."

"Yes, Commander," replied his men in unison.

Linger left them to their task and crossed the courtyard to enter Schleyer's personal chambers. He found him sitting in the near darkness, flanked by an armed sentry. Schleyer was dabbing his eyes in defeat—probably mourning the death of Gabrielle Reinmaul. Linger ordered the soldier to help his fellow troops. When the man was gone, the merc leader closed the door and whirled to face Schleyer. He stared through the sniffling businessman, and Schleyer's true persona finally came to light.

"Quit your sniveling, you pathetic shit," Linger growled.

Schleyer turned a surprised look on his subordinate. "What did you say?"

"You heard me," Linger said. "We have no time for this. Belasko is undoubtedly preparing to assault the complex in Frankfurt. We must get there first and mount a counteroffensive."

"It is hopeless," Schleyer said with a wave. "We do not have enough troops to continue with the operation, and the fighter will never see completion before Belasko attacks. Our best chance to make it through this alive is to pack up and move the operation. We must begin again in another place."

Fury rose inside Linger's throat, manifesting itself in a flurry of curse words. Schleyer leaned back in his chair, a shudder of fear running through his body. After calming himself, Linger reached inside his leather jacket and withdrew his Mauser 80SAV. He pointed the pistol at Schleyer's head, his eyes burning with hate.

"Many of my men have died today because of your carelessness," Linger said. "Now you wish to abandon our plans for the sake of running away from Belasko, your tail tucked between your legs. You are a worthless swine and a coward. We will proceed with this operation, and you will stand your ground with the rest of us. Otherwise, I will personally kill you here and now. Do you understand me?"

"Who do you think you are?"

"I am a soldier, willing to die in battle if need be, but you, Edel Schleyer, are no god. You are not even a leader. You do not have the first clue what it means to be a leader. I will no longer tolerate your childish whims. My men, *real* men, have sacrificed themselves on the field of battle for me, and for the honor of the Iron Skull. Do not think you will spit upon that sacrifice and grind their blood under your feet. I will kill you and consider I have done my men a service."

Schleyer rose suddenly and clenched his fists. "You cannot do this!"

"Yes, I can...and I will, if you test my patience. You are the only one with the resources to rebuild the Iron Skull, and restore my honor. I will have those resources at my disposal, or I will shoot you in the heart and hang your body from the highest point in the country. You will hang in effigy for all others to see. They will know then how foolish you were to think you could contend with me and win. Now, we shall go to Frankfurt."

"I swear, Linger, that *you* will be the one to hang."

"I do not think so. From here on out, I am assuming command of the operation. You will do as I instruct you to do. Should you entertain the idea of disobedience, I will execute you without questions. Move!"

Linger waved the pistol with a snap of his wrist. Edel Schleyer raised his hands obediently and complied.

BOLAN AND HIS COMPANIONS marched the last mile to the autobahn, abandoning the half track behind a deep brush line, invisible to passersby on the country road. Bolan had field-stripped the M-16 and tucked it—along with his grenade satchel, remaining C-4 and the pistols—into the HK21-E's protective case, which had been lying on the rear floorboards of the half track.

An elderly woman stopped and picked them up as they

made their way down the shoulder of the autobahn. In broken German, Bolan explained Krizova's wounds had come from an auto accident off the highway, and the woman seemed satisfied. The Executioner hadn't bothered to explain his and Grimaldi's odd dress. There wouldn't have been any point, since none of the fugitives understood much German to begin with. The story seemed more convincing when Bolan asked the woman to deposit them in front of the first police station in town.

After the old woman pulled away, Bolan led the trio down the street to the U-Bahn station. One changeover and an hour later, the weary combatants arrived at Bolan's hotel. After a quick snack of the leftovers prepared by Kaufmann, Bolan drew Krizova a hot bath and put antiseptic on her wounds. He tucked her into bed and returned to the small table in the studio-style kitchen.

Bolan could see Grimaldi eyeing him warily as he poured himself a cup of coffee and collapsed in the chair across from his friend. Bolan hadn't spoken of Jütta Kaufmann since their escape from the fortress. The pilot wasn't about to force the issue, so he turned the conversation to more immediate matters.

"How are you planning to get inside that underground hangar, Sarge?"

"I've been thinking that over since we left the fortress, and I still don't have any easy answers. The only way to get in there will be the same way I made entry the first time."

"Won't they have it guarded?" Grimaldi queried.

"Probably, but that's where you come in. I'm going to need a diversion."

"What type?"

Bolan sipped his coffee before continuing. "It looks like we've got about two pounds of C-4 left. Not enough to blow a hole in that steel access door, but it is enough to make some noise. Schleyer's actually going to help slit his own throat, and he doesn't even know it yet.''

"Schleyer?" Grimaldi asked with skepticism in his voice. "You still think he'll try to get the fighter out of here, after all the trouble you've caused him?"

"He's been predictable so far," the Executioner reminded him. "The guy has too much invested in this project to give up now. If they still want to launch on time, even if it's just to take the prototype to a secured location and start again, they'll have to defend the place. I'm relying on this fact to make the plan work.''

"Then what?"

"Once you've created the diversion, I'll maneuver inside and clear a path. It shouldn't be too difficult. Krizova told me the Iron Skull's force had numbered maybe one hundred troops. Apparently, I took a big chunk out of that when they kept sending them after me.''

"Sounds like a fair assumption. What do you want me to do?''

"Your goal will be to get yourself and the Krizovas out of there. If the plane isn't operational, you take Krizova and Mila and get out of Germany. Once you have my signal, you get out. Don't wait for me. I mean it, Jack.''

"I understand, Sarge," Grimaldi said.

"For the moment, we'll rest here. The fighter is scheduled to be completed at dawn. That's when I want to be ready. We'll take turns on the couch. I think we're pretty secure here, but I want to be ready for every possible scenario. I'll take first watch, clean up these weapons some. We'll trade in four-hour increments.''

BOLAN PRESSED HIMSELF flat to the cool stone as movement ahead caught his eye. The dark train tunnel was as damp and cold as it had been when he'd last entered. He watched the two sentries ahead, trying to ignore the uncomfortable rock sticking into him through his blacksuit. One of the sentries turned and disappeared in the opposite direction, while the other seemed to continue nearer. A minute later, the process was reversed, and seemed to repeat itself. It was a roving patrol—a lucky break for Bolan.

The Executioner checked the luminous dial of his watch. He let the rounds go on for several minutes, timing each one. It took an average of two minutes for the roving patrol members to contact one another. Bolan waited until the next one had passed, then rose from the shadows and took the first sentry from behind. Wrapping one arm around the merc's neck in a choke hold, he then pushed the guy's head in the opposite direction with his other arm, breaking the guys neck. He eased the corpse to the ground.

Bolan moved down the tunnel, hugging the walls. The second sentry met the same fate, but the soldier's time had run out. A third man saw the shadow of struggle and turned to run for the branching hallway leading to the watchtower. Bolan took off in pursuit, but there was no way he could get inside softly. The only way to keep his plan from falling apart was to order Grimaldi to blow the plastique the soldier had attached to the entryway off the launch tunnel earlier that morning.

He keyed his radio microphone. "Do it, Eagle!"

Bolan could hear the poppings of the C-4 as each one blew in succession. He watched as the sentry went past the adjoining corridor. Where was he going? The soldier raised the M-16 and pulled the trigger. The rounds ricocheted off the stone walls as the man rounded a slight curve in the tunnel. Bolan continued his pursuit, but stopped short when he took the corner. The tunnel simply dropped off. The edges around the square opening were reinforced, with an observation railing mounted to them. The tunnel opened onto a bird's-eye view of the entire operation.

The gunman whirled to fire on Bolan and simultaneously

began to yell a warning over the side. However, the explosions had seemed to divert most attention up the launch tunnel and masked the noise from Bolan's M-16 as he shot the gunman through vital organs. The merc flipped over the railing and fell to the cold, hard stone thirty feet below.

Bolan crossed the tunnel to the observation platform and looked out on the scene. The fighter appeared completely. Its matte-black airframe stood out starkly against the lighter walls of gray stone that surrounded it. It was truly a monument to modern aeronautical design. The body was slim, with a head and nose cone shaped similar to that of an eagle. Four wings jutted from her sides, and the huge cannons and weaponry mounted to her frame were an awesome testament to weapons of mass destruction.

But was she ready to fly?

Bolan could see Krizova standing under one of the wings, seeking cover as troops moved around him, heading toward the entrance to the launch tunnel. The soldier popped in an incendiary grenade and fired, aiming for the bulk of the troops. The grenade showered white phosphorus in their midst, and Bolan immediately followed the incendiary with an HE round. The underground complex seemed to rock with explosions.

Bolan began sniping the soldiers one by one, bringing the count up to ten more dead terrorists. The Iron Skull had truly been whittled down. The diversion had worked. The remaining mercs saw the futility of their situation and rushed up the launch tunnel, intent on making their escape through the far entrance. Within seconds, the launch bay was empty, except for Dr. Vasec Krizova.

"Dr. Krizova?" Bolan shouted.

The Czech scientist looked up to see Bolan standing on the observation deck. "Mr. Belasko! I am so happy to see you!"

"Is that fighter operational?" Bolan demanded.

"Yes, it is completed. Would you like me to destroy it?"

"Not unless you want to shred your only ticket out of here. Wait there!"

Bolan turned and walked back to the access corridor. He passed through the watchtower and descended the ladder to ground level. Krizova appeared delighted to see him, but the soldier had no time for happy reunions.

"Get in that plane and get her ready. A friend of mine will be arriving soon. You're going to help him fly that thing out of here."

"Mr. Belasko, I do not mean to argue, but have you kept your end of the bargain?"

"Your daughter is safe, Doctor," Bolan replied, "and she'll be leaving with you. Just do as I say. We're taking that fighter out of here."

"I am afraid not, Herr Belasko."

The Executioner spun on his heel, turning in the direction of the familiar voice. Dortmund Linger stepped from the shadows of an alcove, a Mauser 80SAV clutched in his left hand. Bolan knew he couldn't bring the M-16 to bear in time without getting both himself and Krizova killed. Far ahead and echoing back down through the launch tunnel, the sound of hydraulics signaled the opening of the entrance door to the complex.

"Sounds like your crew has bailed, Linger. Maybe you ought to join them before I decide to kill you."

"Really, Herr Belasko?" Linger replied. His deep voice boomed with laughter in the poor acoustics of the complex. "I think you are mistaken. It is I who will kill you."

"I owe you, Linger. For the deaths of Carter Wiley and Jütta Kaufmann."

"Really? That is most amusing. I am the one in control here," Linger stated, gesturing for Bolan to surrender his weapon.

"Maybe I'll collect—maybe someone else will. Eventually, though, your tab will be called and it will be time to pay up.''

"That sounds almost poetic.'' Linger tossed the pistol away and drew a combat knife from his belt. He crouched into an experienced stance and added, "Let us see if you are as fine a soldier as you are a poet. Come to me, Belasko. See if you can make me pay.''

Thinking of Kaufmann and how she'd died with honor, Bolan knew he had to repay that debt with similar honor. He set his M-16 aside. Linger lunged forward. He feinted a slash maneuver toward Bolan's gut, but swept his arm up at the last second and nicked the soldier's shoulder. The Executioner danced away, barely avoiding serious injury. Linger was unbelievably fast for his size, and Bolan was unarmed. His opponent was obviously experienced with the use of a knife. Linger was playing with him, taunting him as the two combatants circled each other.

The Executioner decided he would play his own game.

Linger feinted again, but Bolan was ready this time. The merc lunged for a straight stab at the belly, then swooped the knife over his head in an attempt to bury the blade in Bolan's chest. The Executioner blocked the overhead slash with his forearm while launching a front kick to his opponent's groin. Linger twisted sideways, taking the point of Bolan's steel-tipped boots on his hip. The blow was staggering, and the man fell backward over an empty crate.

The soldier rushed forward in an attempt to disarm his opponent, but Linger was ready for such a move. He tossed Bolan over his head with a judo circle throw, and the Executioner landed hard on the other side, the wind knocked from his lungs. He got to his feet and spun to face his enemy.

Linger edged slowly to his feet, favoring his other hip. "You are good, Belasko. You are very good. I am impressed.''

Bolan said nothing, simply watching for Linger's next move. It came almost immediately in the form of a roundhouse kick, which Bolan deflected by twisting his body inward and curling his arms around Linger's leg. He locked Linger's leg in a viselike hold, then kicked the free leg out from under him at the knee. Linger screamed in agony as the tendons in his knee ripped. He slashed helplessly at his opponent, but the Executioner now had the upper hand. He stretched Linger's leg to one side and kicked the man in the groin. Linger roared in pain, now waving the knife frantically in a desperate attempt to score a hit.

Bolan reached out and grabbed Linger's wrist. He twisted outward and rammed his knee into the man's arm at the elbow. The knife fell from numbed fingers, but Linger had no time left to contemplate his suffering. The Executioner dropped down to one knee, landing on his adversary's solar plexus, and drove a rigid hand into his throat. Cartilage was crushed under the impact of Bolan's rock-hard knuckles, effectively smashing the windpipe and lacerating the esophagus.

Linger began to choke on his own vomit and blood as Bolan rose and studied the dying man dispassionately. The city of Frankfurt would be a little safer tonight as it slept. Linger had been responsible for the deaths of fine individuals like Carter Wiley and Jütta Kaufmann, and hundreds more just like them. He had killed innocents, declaring himself a hero in a war schemed up by his own imagination.

It was a fitting end.

Bolan was retrieving his weapons as Grimaldi arrived with Mila Krizova in tow. Father and daughter hugged each other tightly.

"Ready to get out of here?" Bolan asked.

"You bet," Grimaldi replied with a smile, clapping his hand on his friend's shoulder.

"Then get moving," Bolan said. "And don't forget to finish that castle on your way out of town."

"Understood."

The men turned wordlessly from each other, and Bolan began a room-to-room search of the complex as Grimaldi and the Krizovas prepared for their departure. Only the echo of his footsteps greeted Bolan in the empty corridors. He moved along the complex, checking each room and cubicle, searching every corner.

He was searching for one final detail.

Perhaps Edel Schleyer had escaped with the fleeing mercenaries, although Bolan didn't find that likely. It was possible he had remained at the castle, which would explain his absence. Then again, something was gnawing at Bolan. Something in his gut instinct told him Schleyer was there somewhere in the complex. As Bolan pushed through another door and found himself in a darkened office, he no longer had to wonder.

Schleyer was motionless with his head resting on a desk. Bolan quickly found the light switch. Pink-and-red splotches decorated the wall to Schleyer's left. Bolan didn't have to guess what had happened. An antique Walther PPK was clutched in the man's right fist. The soldier stared unemotionally at Schleyer's body as the roar of the jet's engines reached his ears. He could feel the rumbling of the complex as the fighter left from the hangar and sped up the launch tunnel. The echoes began to die, the only telltale sign the plane had even existed.

A moment later, the complex fell silent.

"Wooooo-haaaaaa!" Grimaldi yelped, feeling himself pressed into the seat as the K-1 jet fighter made its way over the German countryside. "This is one bad ship, Doc!"

"Um, thank you, I think," Krizova replied. "The targets you selected on the map are coming up. I have the grid locked in, and weapons are released to your command. Remember, you must slow in order to achieve lock.''

"Then let's finish this business!" Grimaldi announced through the headset in his shiny silver flight helmet. "On my mark.''

The computerized topographical map flashed in front of Grimaldi at almost unreadable speeds, but the pilot kept decreasing the throttle to make sure he didn't overshoot the target. Krizova was sitting immediately behind him in the navigator's seat, and Mila took up the rear in what would have been the bombardier's chair. Krizova had designed the fighter to allow for navigation and weapons systems to be controlled from any position, but flight was controlled only from the pilot or navigation chair.

Grimaldi held the fighter on course until a beeping sounded in his ear and he saw a red flash on his LCD targeting screen.

"There is your target!" Krizova cried through his headset. "Fire! Fire!''

Grimaldi flipped the safety switch and triggered the weapons array. He stabbed his firing switches in succession, and three AIM-9L Sidewinders sped from the fighter's underbelly. Grimaldi opened the throttle, pulling away as he detected the flash of the missiles exploding in his periphery. The red flashing immediately turned to green, and Krizova's voice was ecstatic through the headseats, nearly blowing out Jack's eardrums.

"You did it! You did it!" Krizova screamed.

"No, Dr. Krizova," Grimaldi replied with a smile, loosening his chin strap. He punched in the GPS transponder code, which would find the nearest U.S. aircraft carrier. "You did it.''

EPILOGUE

Dan Lincoln entered his pitch-dark office in downtown Frankfurt.

He didn't bother to turn on the lights or secure the door behind him. Lincoln rushed to the file drawers, lighting his miniflashlight and holding it between his teeth. He produced a large paper bag from inside his coat and began dumping the files into the bag. When he was finished emptying the three drawers, he dropped the bag in the center of the room. Lincoln whipped out a small can of lighter fluid and a cigarette lighter. He began to soak the files, then squirted the fluid up the side of the walls until the can was empty.

The Executioner had seen enough.

Bolan stepped from the alcove behind Lincoln and snapped on the desktop lamp. Lincoln jumped away from the fuel-soaked bag, a mixture of guilt and surprise pasted across his features. He froze when he saw the muzzle of the Beretta pistol staring back at him.

"Leaving so soon, Lincoln?" Bolan asked, his eyes narrowing accusingly.

"Belasko? What the fuck are you doing here?"

"I might ask you the same question," Bolan replied icily, "although we both know the answer to that."

"Now look, man, I wasn't going to fry you. Schleyer wanted me to issue a contract on you, you know, to reach out to all my connections." Lincoln chuckled nervously.

"But I'm not the telephone company. I told him no way. I don't need that."

"It's a bit late for that, isn't it?" Bolan asked. "You should have thought of that before you sent Carter Wiley to his death."

"Hey, look, man. I didn't know that crazy man Linger was gonna off him, you know?"

"You don't know much of anything," Bolan growled. "Linger and Schleyer are dead."

"What?"

"You're next."

As Lincoln scrambled to open his desk drawer, Bolan squeezed the trigger, and the 9 mm subsonic round punched a hole in the center of the traitor's forehead. The man stood straight up a moment, a look of complete shock spreading across his features before he dropped to the floor. Bolan holstered his pistol as he stepped forward and retrieved the lighter. Nothing angered him more than traitors to his country. America wasn't perfect, but she was all Bolan had. Lincoln had just been another scum who had fallen to the whims of money, luxury and power—three things that could suck the freedom right from an individual.

"The only real freedom we have is choice, Lincoln," Bolan whispered. "You made yours."

Bolan struck the wheel of the lighter and touched the flame to the files. He then turned out the desk light and walked calmly to the front door as flames followed the igniter trails across the threadbare carpeted floors and up the walls. He stepped through the vestibule and out into the crisp October air, pulling the collar of his overcoat tight against his ears. As the bitter winds picked up and howled through the buildings of Frankfurt, the Executioner remembered a certain tough and beautiful agent who had died saving his life.

She would join the friendly ghosts.

And he would remember.

Gold Eagle brings you high-tech action and mystic adventure!

#119 Fade to Black

Created by

MURPHY
and SAPIR

Art begins to imitate life in Tinsel Town as real-life events are mirrored in small independent films...and the U.S. President's life is placed in jeopardy.

Available in April 2000 at your favorite retail outlet.

James Axler

OUTLANDERS™

WREATH OF FIRE

Ambika, an amazon female, has been gathering groups of
Outlanders in the Western Isles in an attempt to overthrow
the Barons. But are her motives just a ploy to satisfy her
own ambition?

JAMES AXLER

DEATHLANDS®

Shadow World

Ryan Cawdor must face the threat of invaders that arrive from a parallel earth where the nukecaust never happened. And when he is abducted through a time corridor, he discovers a nightmare that makes Deathlands look tame by comparison!

Shadow THE EXECUTIONER®
as he battles evil for 352 pages of heart-stopping action!

SuperBolan®